Also edited by Robert Bartlett Haas:

*A Primer for the Gradual Understanding
of Gertrude Stein (1971)*

Reflection On The Atomic Bomb (1973)

How Writing Is Written (1974)

VOLUME II OF THE PREVIOUSLY
UNCOLLECTED WRITINGS OF

GERTRUDE STEIN

HOW WRITING
IS WRITTEN

edited by

ROBERT BARTLETT HAAS

1977
BLACK SPARROW PRESS
Santa Barbara

LIBRARY OF CONGRESS CATALOGING IN PUBLICATION DATA

Stein, Gertrude, 1874-1946.
    How writing is written.

    (The previously uncollected writing of Gertrude Stein, v. 2)
    I. Title. II. Series: Stein, Gertrude, 1874-1946. The previously
uncollected writings of Gertrude Stein, v. 2.
PS3537.T323A6 1973 vol. 2   73-17266
ISBN 0-87685-200-2
ISBN 0-87685-199-5 (pbk.)

Third Printing

TABLE OF CONTENTS

The dating of the above works is in all cases the date of composition rather than the date of periodical publication and follows the chronology established by Richard Bridgman in his *Gertrude Stein in Pieces*, Oxford University Press, 1970.

The portrait of Gertrude Stein on the cover of this book is taken from an oil by Pierre Tal-Coat painted in France in 1935. This oil is currently in the collection of Galerie Henri-Bénézit, Paris, and is reproduced with their kind permission.

Preface

GERTRUDE STEIN'S
"SENSE OF THE IMMEDIATE"

Volume I of the Previously Uncollected Writings of Gertrude Stein carried the record of her literary development from her radical "change of style" in 1914 to her mid-career concern with American syntax and "immediate" history. During this two decade span she committed her energies to "direct description."

Notes made by Hal Levy* during a Gertrude Stein lecture (in 1935) indicate how she referred to this process of direct or immediate description: "She has disciplined her mind to the point where she can concentrate on a subject until it, the subject itself, has taken form. Then, dissociating that mental unit from connotative words and meanings, she writes. She doesn't write what her subject matter looks like. She doesn't write how it feels. She doesn't write about it, or at it, or around it. She writes *it*."

That this process was based on a consistent point of view about the dynamic and evolving nature of the world around her, and that she sought to use the English language in a way which revealed this movement may be traced to what she did to avoid the literary conventions of her time and to create newer and more satisfactory approaches to describing, with *integrity*, the multifaceted structure of the dynamic world postulated by her beloved teacher, William James.

When, years later, James visited her studio in Paris, his amazement at her work and the work of the contemporary painters with which she had surrounded herself led him to say, after he had "looked and gasped," "I told you, he said, I always told you that you should keep your mind open."

Gertrude Stein kept her mind open on the subject of her art. She was a writer. She used language as her *métier*. What was the language of integrity in an open world? Her approach was a fresh

---

*The late Hal Levy, teacher of song lyric writing and publisher of popular music in Los Angeles, maintained a lifelong interest in Gertrude Stein. He was one of the publishers of Gertrude Stein's 1941 volume, What Are Masterpieces.

one, as we learn again from Hal Levy's practically verbatim and previously unpublished notes: "The English language has been thrust upon Americans. And it is wrong. As static and immobile as are the English, just so ever-moving are Americans. Here is a huge country. Not a mere island. Naturally people move. And they need a moving language. A language that can interpret American life. Nouns and adjectives won't express American life. They are too weak, too immobile. But verbs, adverbs, prepositions and the like, ah, they are moving, just as Americans. Obviously we cannot suddenly junk the English language and adopt some other tongue. English is too connotative, too close to us. Our problem is to adapt the English language to American needs. To make it move with us Americans. That is the problem—to write things as they are, not as they seem. Our aim must be not to explain things, but to write the thing itself, and thereby in itself be self explanatory."

This kind of thinking led Gertrude Stein to use words and sentences as if she had invented them.

Volume II of the Previously Uncollected Writings of Gertrude Stein contains works from the second half of her writer's career. They move from the most elliptical to the most easily understood. The great "forms" in which she had come to cast her writing and to which she gave new life and significance (narration, the portrait, poetry, the play, the meditation and the explication) had done their work. Later concerns were the autobiography, newer possibilities in the novel, short story or historical piece. In the concluding years of her life, she learned to communicate with her growing public in unique essays and written lectures. Her "way out" areas of final exploration concerned the operational differences between poetry and prose, non-progressive movement, or vibration, the qualitative differences between writing for the self (entity) and writing for the other (identity).

Her overarching interest, however, was not in form but in *content*, and the content of her work was always the content of *the present*—what she found there, how she could put it into words which would not violate its vividness or its uniqueness, its repeated qualities or its absolute uniquenesses.

Her genius as a writer lies in her sense of the immediate. That, for her, was how writing was written.

Robert Bartlett Haas
University of California
Los Angeles, 1973

HOW WRITING IS WRITTEN
Volume Two
Of the Previously Uncollected Writings of
GERTRUDE STEIN

VII

Disembodied Movement

During the late 1920's and early 1930's Gertrude Stein seems to have been dealing with some of the larger reaches of literary theory—what the sentence was, the paragraph, grammar and vocabulary, as seen from the standpoint of an American syntax. Another concern was the description of events by portraying movement so intense as to be a thing in itself, not a thing in relation to something else.

"Grant or Rutherford B. Hayes" attempts to do this by replacing the noun and the adjective and emphasizing the more active parts of speech. Here a driving pulse is created by syncopating the sentence. The thrust comes from a concentrated use of verbs and verb phrases. In 1929 Gertrude Stein had a terrible fight with Bernard Fay over nouns and adjectives. She didn't like them, she said, and he did. She punished him by making his portrait almost entirely of adverbs and prepositions. Something like that is going on with Grant or Rutherford B. Hayes.

"Page IX" may be thought of as a five line poem, or it may be thought of as a structure which shoots out like a sky rocket and then bursts into four timeless light clusters, each triggered by its internal connective "or".

"Prothalamium" was an apparently innocent little lyric until Dr. Virginia Tufte found it contained every major convention of the classical nuptial poetry: the beauty of nature, birds, war and the hope of peace, sanction of marriage as a social or holy institution, and the mystical union. All this Gertrude Stein accomplished in a concentrated three stanza form with a benedictory conclusion. The inner movement of the poem is a quick back and forth which sets up a hum like the vibrating wings of a big queen bee.

All the pieces in this section have to do with movement detached from an outer context and vital within its own parameters.

GRANT OR RUTHERFORD B. HAYES

Grant or Rutherford B. Hayes.
Jump. Once for all. With the praising of. Once for all. As a chance. To win.
Once for all. With a. Chance. To win.
Rutherford B. Hayes.
Grant.
Rutherford B. Hayes. Won.
Grant. Won.
And
They can. Be thoughtful.
Alone. They can. Be thoughtful alone. And they can. Be won. By being. Thoughtful. Alone. They can win. By being. Thoughtful. Alone.
Grant. One.
Be. Is followed. By went.
They went. Very carefully.
Not every minute.
They went. Very carefully. But not. Every minute.
Grant was followed. But not. Every minute.
They went. Grant was followed. They went. Very carefully. But not. Every minute.
There is no ugliness. In women. Rutherford B. Hayes. Or men. Or children. Or women. Grant.
There could be no ugliness. In men. Or children. Rutherford B. Hayes. There could be. No ugliness. Grant. In women. Rutherford B. Hayes. Or Grant.
In women. Grant. There is what with mine. They will. Fix. Their hope. In chairs. For them. A choice. Be well. Rutherford B. Hayes or Grant.
Or. Rutherford B. Hayes. Or Grant.
A simple thing. To say. He knew his name. Which was. Not then. The same. His name.
Or whether. They will. Name him.
Rutherford B. Hayes.
Shares. His. With Some.
Grant is more than. This with some. So much. As much. As some.
Some. Does not leave. With one.

13

Who has Rutherford B. Hayes known.
Just why they leave. Who leaves.
Grant.
Just why. They leave.
But they. Come. To think.
And they will. Think. Or will.
They supply them.
With help. Sometime.
Rutherford B. Hayes. Was colonel and brave.
In youth. How did they. Pronounce it.
Should they be selfish. As a wish.
Rutherford B. Hayes or Grant.
Could Rutherford B. Hayes know.
The difference between snow.
And sand.
Did Rutherford B. Hayes.
Think well of distance.
Rutherford B. Hayes and Grant. Can make confusion.
But not with intelligence.
So some think. That they remember. Rain.
Which is known as cows.
In mud.
Or stones.
In rivers.
By thoughtfulness.
In hopes of him.
He was. A horse.
Without. A show.
Which made them go.
They will say so.
Rutherford B. Hayes has a name.
It is very historical.
Each time. That a list. Is made.
It is. Very historical.
Rutherford B. Hayes or Grant.

He met Rutherford B. Hayes and he met Rutherford B. Hayes
and his mother. Rutherford B. Hayes or Grant. And they wish.
That they had seen them. Or. One. Another.

Rutherford B. Hayes met them and they were there. With one
another, because Rutherford B. Hayes, or Grant, and they met
more. Than. One. Or. Another. Rutherford B. Hayes. Or
Grant.

How many states. Have Indian. Names. How many states have names. For it. Names.

Rutherford B. Hayes. Or Grant. Have names. How. Many states. Have names. Rutherford B. Hayes. Or names. Rutherford B. Hayes. Or Grant. Or names.

How many states have their names. Not states. Have their names. Rutherford B. Hayes. Or Grant.

When he is Grant or Rutherford B. Hayes. One. Hesitates after. He is Rutherford B. Hayes. Or rather. Or Grant. Or rather. Or Rutherford B. Hayes. Now all one needs is a nightingale.

Nobody knows. How many. In a minute. Rutherford B. Hayes. Not any. In a minute.

Rutherford B. Hayes.

Or Grant.

It is why. They call.

It is. Why. They call.

Them. To them.

And they manage. To arrange. A way. To go. Away. To stay.

Rutherford B. Hayes. Or. Grant.

It is easier to like ilex and Rutherford B. Hayes or Grant.

Which. They made. Soothe. It.

Which is. By the time. Of extras.

Rutherford B. Hayes wins Grant.

Or Grant. Rutherford B. Hayes.

Should. They or. Theirs. Be. Justice.

Rutherford B. Hayes.

Or Grant.

Read what they say. Believe it. And see. If. The nuns fall, the nun falls. Nuns. Veiling. Read what they say. If the nuns. Veiling. Is not navy. Blue.

And so. They leave. It. Alone.

Rutherford B. Hayes. Neglects. It. Not more. Than. They. Can. Not. Have it.

And so. Or Grant.

Rutherford B. Hayes. Or Grant.

For them. A feeling. Is. Made. Best. For them.

Nor. May they. The month. Of May.

Which is. Which for her. Is it since.

They seem more. Than able.

To. Sanctify. What. They leave.

To care for. And to try. To be. Earnestly.
Their leaving.
Hiram Ulysses Grant or.
Ulysses Simpson Grant.
Or. Rather.
For. Him. In. Leaving. In. Theirs. Ever.
Rutherford B. Hayes or Grant.
In. Messenger. For. When.
They know.
They also knew. That. They congregate.
For them. To think. Of little things.
In this. Which. They will like. As well.
Rutherford B. Hayes was elected president.
Or Grant. Was elected President.
Rutheford B. Hayes was elected.
President. Or Grant. Was elected.
President. Or Rutherford B. Hayes.
Was elected. President. Or Grant.
Was elected. President.
Grant. Was elected. President.
Twice.
Rutherford B. Hayes was elected.
President. Once.
Or Grant. Was elected. President.
Twice.
Rutherford B. Hayes. Was elected.
President. Once.
Or Grant. Was elected. President.
Twice.
They see. Forty minutes. As once.
They are. Forty. Very. Well. Twice.
Rutherford B. Hayes. Was elected.
President. Once.
Or. Grant. Was. Elected.
President. Twice.
He might. Have been. Elected. President.
Once. He was elected. President.
Twice.
He was elected. President. Once.
He might. Have been. Elected.
President. Twice.
Rutherford B. Hayes. Was.

16

Elected. President. Once.
Or. Grant. Was. Elected. President.
Twice. He might. Have been. Elected.
President. Once. Or. Even. Twice.
Or Grant. Was. Elected. President. Twice.
For. Which. They. Were. Not. Forgotten.
Because. Of this. They have.
Not been. Forgotten.
Or Grant. Was elected. President.
Twice.
For which. They have. Not been.
Forgotten.
For which. Rutherford B. Hayes.
Was elected. President. Once.
All. Who have said. That grass. Is red. Have not. Been
familiar. With clover.
All who. Have said. That there. Is no grass. That is red.
Have not been familiar. With clover.
Four leaf clover.
All. Who have said. That. Grass. Is not red.
Have been. Familiar. With other clover. Than with. Red
clover.
All who have said. That grass is red. Have been. Familiar.
With red clover.
Some clover. Is red.
Some clover. Is four leaf clover.
She is very ready. To look. For four leaf clover.
And find it.
President Rutherford B. Hayes.
Or Grant.
Rutherford B. Hayes. Or Grant.

1931

PAGE IX

I like a half a day on one day
Or a whole day on some day
Or three days on Friday
Or six days on Tuesday
Or forty days and forty nights on Wednesday.

1933

PROTHALAMIUM

Love like anything
In war-time
Day and night
In peace and war-time
Birds are Bobolinks
In war-time
Girls are Louises
In war-time
War-time Peace-time. Two in one. In Peace-time.
Two in one and one in two. In War-time. Louise
and Bobolink are one. In Peace-time in War-time
Peace-time.

They say
How do you do. And we say.
How do you do too.
And they say very well I thank you
Which pleases them
And us too
Two and two that is one is two
Which is you
Louise and Bobolink

Thank you.
They are engaged. To be married.

1939

VIII
Entity

*Works in which Gertrude Stein believed she achieved "entity"
she considered her purest and most lasting contribution. Her fundamental thinking about "entity" and "identity" was embodied in*
The Geographical History of America Or The Relation Of Human
Nature To The Human Mind *(1935). Uncollected pieces which
fit this category are short stories and novellas of a new sort—little
tone poems full of easily discernible themes and patterns of development, which are the outcome of Gertrude Stein's increasing interest in narration (rather than narrative) at this time.*

*"The Superstitions of Fred Anneday . . ." accounts for the first
Fred and his slippery sea-change brothers, who appear in a short
novel of superstitions with three mottos and two Chapter III's.
Gertrude Stein says she "can tell this story as I go. I like to tell a
story so." In doing so, she speculates on the character of the modern novel: "a novel goes as dreams go" . . . "a great many things
that happened" . . . "do not bother about a story". What is immediate cannot be a story, which must be stretched in time from
past to present to future. The novel of the present is proposed here.*

*"A Water-Fall and A Piano" is a mystery story set in a French
village. Without really knowing what happened between Helen
the orphan, the Frenchwoman with the puppies, and the visiting
Englishwoman, we know that the Englishwoman is mysteriously
dead. The trio of women is again completed by an American. Will
she, too, die mysteriously?*

*"Is Dead" deals with another village mystery, spelling out the
clues but leaving the solution up to the reader: "All of us who think
about it see what we see."*

"Butter Will Melt" is a narrative prose portrait of Gertrude Stein's cook, Nyen. She wrote about him in Everybody's Autobiography. The Atlantic Monthly *thought this piece of writing was "delectable", so they printed it.* "... and if it is", *wrote Gertrude Stein,* "it was because it was like his cooking."

"The Autobiography of Rose" was a study for the later children's book, The World is Round *(1938).* Gertrude Stein once wrote that the only poetry in war-time is children, and this work provides an example. Onto Rose Gertrude Stein projected her bothersome problems of entity and identity: "She knows her name is Rose because they call her Rose." Like the "I am I because my little dog knows me" of Mother Goose, Rose has a sense of audience and thus a sense of identity.

"Ida" is the short novella which was extended into Ida A Novel *(1940).* A heroine who does almost nothing, but manages to fill her day. A heroine who became so famous, "Everybody knew about her." Then there are two Idas—the non-remembering Ida who has moments of entity and no audience, and the other Ida who has moments of identity and has an audience to admire her. Anyone who has read The Geographical History *(1935) or* What Are Masterpieces *(1935) or* The Mother of Us All *(1945-1946) will recognize that Gertrude Stein is wrestling with what her own experience of fame and fortune had done to the quality of her writing.*

THE SUPERSTITIONS OF FRED ANNEDAY, ANNDAY, ANDAY
A NOVEL OF REAL LIFE

A cuckoo bird is singing in a cuckoo tree, singing to me oh singing to me.

It was many years before it happened that that song was written and sung but it did happen.

A cuckoo bird did come and sit in a tree close by and sing, sing cuckoo to me.

And this is the way it came to happen.

As I say the song was written and sung many years before, before this happening.

The song was written and sung in Italy.

There Fred Annday was living in a villa in Fiesole. He had been born and raised in America had Fred Anday and there in America he had naturally never heard a cuckoo sing although he had heard a cuckoo clock sing.

And when he first heard a cuckoo sing cuckoo, and that was in Germany he was convinced that it was a clock and not a bird and it took a great deal of argument to convince him that it really was a bird and that birds did sing cuckoo.

Then a number of years afterwards in Italy and he was thinking then of one he loved and one who loved him and he did not see a cuckoo and perhaps he did not hear a cuckoo sing but he made the song, a cuckoo bird in sitting in a cuckoo tree singing to me oh singing to me.

And then many years after in France he was thinking of how pleasant it is to be rich and he had as a matter of fact for him a fair amount of money in his pocket and all of a sudden he heard a cuckoo at a distance and he was pleased because he had money in his pocket and if you hear the first cuckoo of the season and there is money in your pocket it means that you will have money for all that year.

And then the miracle happened. The cuckoo came and did what cuckoos never do and it came and sat in a tree right close to him and he could see it and it could see him and it gave a single loud cuckoo and flew away. And this was the beginning of something for him because from that time on he was successful and he believed in superstition yes he did.

Fred Anneday knew all that and he knew better than that. He knew something else about the cuckoo. The cuckoo is a bird who occupies other birds' nests. Perhaps that is the reason he brings money and success. Because he certainly does.

And Fred Anday knew that there was a monastery where there had been monks and the monks had been forced to leave and others who were not monks had taken their place and the neighborhood gathered around at night and made cuckoo noises around the place at night. Cuckoo they said and they meant that the cuckoo takes other birds' nests and that is what these people had done. And so Fred Anneday's life was based on superstition and he was right.

What had Fred Anday done all his life.

A novel is what you dream in your night sleep. A novel is not waking thoughts although it is written and thought with waking thoughts. But really a novel goes as dreams go in sleeping at night and some dreams are like anything and some dreams are like something and some dreams change and some dreams are quiet and some dreams are not. And some dreams are just what any one would do only a little different always just a little different and that is what a novel is.

And this is what a novel is.

Fred Anneday all his life had loved not only one woman not only one thing not only managing everything, not only being troubled so that he could not sleep, not only his mother and religion, not only being the oldest and nevertheless always young enough, not only all this but all his life he had loved superstition and he was right.

He had a great deal to do with everything. This was not only because he was one and the eldest of a very large family which he was but it was because he did have a great deal to do with anything.

One of his friends was Brim Beauvais but he met him later later even than when he loved the only woman whom he ever loved and who was larger and older. And he did not meet Brim Beauvais through her although he might have. It made him think of nightingales. Everything made him think of nightingales and express these thoughts.

If any one is the youngest of seven children and likes it he does not care to hear about birth control because supposing he had not been. If one is the eldest of eight children and likes it he too does not care to hear about birth control but then any one knowing him would know what he would say if any one asked him.

25

If any one is an only child and likes it well then he is an only child and likes it as men or women, or as children. And they may or may not like birth control. There you are that is the answer and even superstition is not always necessary. But really it is. Of course really it is.

Fred Anneday loved a woman and it made all the difference in his life not only that but that he continued to have a great deal to do with everything only it worried him less that is to say not at all and he slept well, that is after he had found that he loved this woman.

Oh Fred Anneday how many things have happened, more than you can say. And Brim Beauvais how many things have happened to Brim Beauvais. Not so many although he thought as many did. And this goes to show how many have told how many so. And this was because Brim Beauvais did not have to count for superstition. Which is a mistake.

Fred Annday was not tall be he changed and his forehead was high. And he changed.

Brim Beauvais was fat that is to say he grew fatter which was not fair as he had been very good looking when he was thin.

Fred Anday loved one woman and she had had a strange thing happen. Not that he loved her for that but it was that which brought them together.

Listen it is very strange. But first how long has Anday lived. About thirty-eight years. And how was he feeling then. Very badly because he was very nervous and did not sleep and his mother was older and thinner and active and wore a wig but bowed as he did.

The woman that he loved was not at all like that although some men love to love a woman who might have looked like their mother if she had looked like that.

There had been a great many women in the life of Fred Anday before he loved the only woman whom he ever loved. First there was his mother.

If there where they lived there had been a mother's day she would have celebrated it eight times and Fred Anday the eldest always would have been there. He would have taken care that he was there with her to celebrate it with and for her.

What does he say and what does she say or what does she say and what does he say.

Another man was Enoch Mariner and he had a beard and violet eyes and stood and looked at one place any time a long time.

26

He said to her to the mother of Fred you are sixty but if everything is alright and it is it is not too late to take a lover. Did she Mrs. Anneday think he meant her. He certainly did and said so. But nobody knew because she never told and besides her sister had just died. This did not interest Enoch Mariner. Enoch Mariner was about forty-one years old at that time.

So now there are three men and there are also more than as many women and there had been as many children.

Fred Annday had no child nor did most of his sisters and his brothers. One had a child just one and only had one child just one.

Brim Beauvais never had a child. His sister had.

Enoch Mariner never had a child and he had no brothers and no sisters to have one.

So there you have a great many things that happened and remember what a novel is it is just that.

And now every one wishes to see any one see the family Annday although a great many were very cross about them. They thought they exaggerated being what they were and that everybody had to say or do something about Fred Annday. Which once he loved the only woman he ever loved slowly nobody did. And this in a way ceased to be exciting. But the way it came about was very exciting as exciting as Dillinger and almost as many knew about it that is if you remember the size of their town and country.

A Motto.

How could it be a little whatever he liked.

CHAPTER II

It is impossible perfectly impossible to mention everybody with whom Anday had something to do. And why. Because there are so many of them. This is true of every one and therefore that is not what a novel is. A novel is like a dream at night where in spite of everything happening any one comes to know relatively few persons. And superstition. Superstition does not come in in dreaming. But in waking oh yes in waking and being waking oh yes it is nothing but superstition. And that is right. That is the way it should be. And anybody likes what they like and anybody likes superstition and so did Fred Anday and the only woman he loved but not in the same way. She was not superstitious in his way and he was not superstitious in her way. But he was right right to be superstitious. Oh yes he was.

What is superstition.

Superstition is believing that something means anything and that anything means something and that each thing means a particular thing and will mean a particular thing is coming. Oh yes it does.

Fred Annday has been superstitious as a little boy. Which of course he had not better not.

Brim Beauvais was superstitious but it moved slowly and as well as not he was not.

Enoch Mariner was superstitious and if he was nobody came to ask him to like it. He liked whatever he did or did not like. He was not very alike. And he made no reference to a wound in his stomach which he had had.

And in this town was a hotel and this at any rate is so. In this town there was a hotel and there was a hotel keeper and his wife and his four children three boys and a girl and his mother and his father and his maiden sister and a governess for the daughter and a woman who helped manage everything and she was a sister of Fred Annday. She came very near being older than Fred only she was not although she felt herself to be in spite of the fact that she had an older sister who still was not older but younger than Fred for Fred after all was the older. Any superstition will help. And it did. He was the eldest and he was older. He knew to a day how he came to be there to stay.

It is not at all confusing to live every day and to meet everyone not at all confusing but to tell any one yes it is confusing even if only telling it to any one how you lived any one day and met everybody all of that day. And now what more can one do than that.

And doing more than that is this.

A Motto.

Once. It is always excited to say twice.
He came twice and she coughed.

CHAPTER III

Now I need no reason to wonder if he went to say farewell. But he never did. Fred Anday never said farewell to any one in a day no one ever does because every one sees every one every day which

28

is a natural way for a day to be. Think of any village town or city or desert island or country house or anything. Of course no dream is like that because after all there has to be all day to be like that. And all day is like that. And there cannot be a novel like that because it is too confusing written down if it is like that so a novel is like a dream when it is not like that.

But what is this yes what is this. It is this.

Now having gotten a little tired of Fred Anday but not of Mariner let us begin with the hotel and the hotel keeper. Everybody can go on talking about Fred Anday at any time. When two or three or ten people are together and you ask them what are they talking about they say oh about Fred Anday and some people are like that. They just naturally are the subject of discussion although everybody has said everything about that one and yet once again everybody begins again. What is the mystery of Fred Anday. Any conversation about him is a conversation about him. That is the way it is. Does he know it. Well I do not know that he does. And if he does it does not add to his superstitions. And about that he is right it does not add to his superstitions.

How could Enoch Mariner have loved more than one woman, of course he did and could. He could even very well remember asking the first woman he asked to marry him. Not only he remembered but also everybody who saw the letter and quite a few did see it because the girl proposed to was so surprised that she had to show it to several of her friends to help her bear it.

She was going to be a school teacher and she and Enoch had met once. He sat down the next day so he said in his letter and took off his coat and he got all ready and he wrote her this letter. He said he knew she would not say yes but she would if he had said all he had to say. And he did say all he had to say and she said no. That is the way life began for Enoch and many years later any one would have married him but he was a bachelor and he had a beard and he walked well and he always proposed to any one to be their lover but was he, this nobody knows.

See how very well Fred Anday might have come to know him but as a matter of fact did he I am not at all sure that he did. And if one were to ask Fred Anday, he would not remember.

A Motto.

Pens by hens.

29

Slowly he felt as he did.

So many things happen that nobody knows that it is necessary to say that he was right to have his superstitions. Of course he is. What is the use of knowing what has happened if one is not to know what is to happen. But of course one is to know what is to happen because it does. Not like it might but might it not happen as it does of course it does. And Anday Fred Anday is never in tears. Not in consequence but never in tears.

And yet Fred Anday could be treated as if he should be in tears but he was not because he had other things. He always did have other things even when it was not true that he slept.

And best of all he knew how he did. He did it very well. And because of this they knew how to say so.

Every one said Anday was not like a hill or like a ball. They said he was not well to do but he had everything to do and he did everything. Nobody could look better than best at that.

For how many reasons was Anday loved or if not loved. Just for how many reasons. Anybody can and could tell just for how many reasons.

And just for how many reasons is a chinaman loved if he comes from Indo China. Just for how many reasons.

Just for how many reasons is everybody loved or please just for how many reasons. Best of all let this be an introduction to how they feel when they do not remember anybody's first name.

One remembers only the names one has heard.

Motto.

Why should he go with him when he stays here for him.

CHAPTER IV

Do not bother. Do not bother about a story oh do not bother. Inevitably one has to know how a story ends even if it does not. Fred Annday's story does not end but that is because there is no more interest in it. And in a way yes in a way that is yes that is always so. I can tell this story as I go. I like to tell a story so.

Anybody will have to learn that novels are like that.

1934

A WATER-FALL AND A PIANO

There are so many ways in which there is no crime.
A goat comes into this story too.
There is always coincidence in crime.

Helen was an orphan that is to say her mother was put away and her father the major was killed in the war.

He went to the war to be killed in the war because his wife was crazy. She behaved strangely when she went to church. She even behaved strangely when she did not. She played the piano and at the same time put cement between the keys so that they would not sound. You see how easy it is to have cement around.

I have often noticed how easy it is to have cement around. Everywhere there are rocks and so everywhere if you have the necessary building and equipment you have cement.

So the mother was put away and the father was dead and the girl was an orphan.

She went to stay where there was a water-fall. Somewhere there some one had two beautiful dogs that were big. One of them was a male and the other was a female, they were to have puppies, their owner a woman wealthy and careful too always wore carpenter's trousers and carpenter's shirts and loved to work. She said when the puppies came there would be nine and they would need more milk than their mother had. She said this was always so. So she said she would buy a goat.

It is difficult to buy a goat not that goats are really rare, but they are not here and there.

A veterinary who could save lives dogs' lives, cows' lives, sheep's lives and even goats' lives he was not so good about horses, because his father and his grandfather had been veterinaries, even his sister always knew what to do, was asked to find a goat a healthy goat. He found one, the goat had been bought and paid for and then no one would let the goat go. This often happens.

Do you see how the whole place was ready now for anybody to be dead.

With them lived an Englishwoman, this was all in France, and the rest were French.

The more you see how the country is the more you do not won-

31

der why they shut the door. They the women do in a way and yet if they did not it would be best.

There are many places where every one is married even in the country, some of them are not. Think of it even in the country some of them are not.

The Englishwoman was not. She was not married. The French women either had been or were going to be, but the Englishwoman never had been nor was going to be.

She took care of the gardens and chickens and the nine puppies when they came and she did without the goat, and then she went away for a month's holiday and then she came back.

In the meantime well not in the meantime because they had always known each other the orphan stayed with the lady who had the nine puppies.

Nobody refuses fear. Not only for themselves but for their dreams because water as if it were a precipice in the moon-light can not disturb because of there being no origin in their dreams.

The Englishwoman came back. She was very cheerful and had seen all her friends and had plans for the nine puppies and the rest of the garden.

Then the dogs found her. She had put her cap beside her and there were two bullets in her head and she was dead.

The police disturbed her they had no business to, the protestant pastor buried her he had no business to, because nobody had been told what had happened to her.

The doctor said nobody could shoot themselves twice. All the doctors said that. An officer said that this was not so. During the war when an officer wanted to be dead he often put a bullet into his head. But it was very often true, that he did not succeed in doing more than putting a bullet into his scalp and then he sent a second one after.

Anyway she was dead, and her family she had a family in England were not satisfied they were satisfied that she was dead oh yes they were satisfied as to that. And the character of the lady who had the nine puppies she kept them all changed and remained changed ever after. And the orphan married an officer.

And every one still talks about it all but not so much now as they did. An American comes to visit in place of the Englishwoman but she has not come to be dead.

1936

IS DEAD

A hotel in the country is not the same as a hotel in a town but it is in a small town. They all went to the funeral. They passed up near the corpse, they kissed the cross, they were sprayed by the censer and they passed near where they the five of them, perhaps more were standing. It was not terrible.

They find likely that she was dead. She fell upon the pavement of cement in the court and broke her back but did not die nor did she know why. In five days she was dead.

Do you see what I mean.

In a hotel one cooks and the other looks at everything. That makes a man and wife.

Everybody knows all that. As that can keep everybody busy, nobody goes out. He did not go out because his mother had not, though his father had. He was like that. She his wife did not go out because she was the only wife he had. He said he did not want another even if she cried. He did not say he did not want another one even if she tried and died.

Oh dear. We all cried. When we heard she was dead. Not that anybody minded. But they said. She is dead.

How did she die. Now I will try. To tell. How she fell. And she was dead. Not at once. But in five days. Although many wanted to send flowers, in case, that she was, already dead.

How can she die if it is not right to die. In some countries nobody can die if it is not right to be dead. And if it happens where nobody dies if it is not right to die, it is a dishonor, that if she is dead, she died.

In every country there is some way in which it is not right to be dead, that is to die. And why. Each one knows why.

Listen to this one.

Long ago that is before this was, long ago, not so very long ago after all because she was not forty, but any way some time ago there was a hotel keeper who had succeeded his father, who had succeeded his father, who had already succeeded his father. In other words if there was to be a son and there came to be three, there would then have been six generations of hotel keepers.

Six generations in some countries are not so many but still any way they are quite a few. It was the sixth who was not yet a hotel keeper and perhaps never would be one because he was to be a lawyer who said that there were six. But he became one that is he became a hotel keeper and the reason why is this.

He was not yet a lawyer when his mother, yes it was his mother, it was she who was found dead, and not in her bed, not even dead anywhere.

Remember the cement was there and she had fallen there and they had put her away from there and it was early in the morning and so nobody who was staying in the hotel knew that she had been there.

It was his mother who was dead there where no one should be dead, when all is said, and very much is said, is always said.

And so he would not be a lawyer because, and this is natural, if a mother is dead, mysteriously dead, a son cannot be trusted as a lawyer, but he can be trusted as a cook, and hotel keeper or as a brother of a cook and hotel keeper, or as a son of a cook and hotel keeper or even later as a grandson and a father of a cook and hotel keeper.

Do you really understand.

Way back before this war, there was a hotel keeper, a very little man with very fine features and if he became very stout later he would be impressive, which he did, and which he was.

He saw a young girl who was also small but rather flat of face who had a smile and who also later on would be stout but she would be stout and charming and be stout and steadily moving in every direction. She would be occupied with every little thing that she ever saw. She would know about clean linen, about peaches and little cakes, as few as possible of each and yet always enough. She would oversee the maids at work, she would push them gently forward to do what there was to do and there was always all of that to do. For them and for her. All day and every day. She was always very nearly perfect when she stood. She never sat. Except when it was late and he and she would dine.

Think of all that.

Just think of all that.

He, the cook and hotel keeper, was little like his mother. His father had been and was tall.

All of us who think about it see what we see.

And then the war came, this late war.

She had come from poorer people than he. He had not come from poor people at all. His father and his grandfather and his grandfather's father had been cooks and hotel keepers and he had not come from poor people at all. She had. This does make a dif-

34

ference and in a way does not make anybody glad.

When the war came he went away to the war. He was a little man and he went away to the war.

Sometimes a little man does not go to the war because he is too little to carry all a soldier has to carry on him, but this man was a little man, and he went to the war and what is more, he did not go and cook at the war, as many a cook did, he went to the war and he fought in the war, and what is more, he fought all the long years of the war until there was no more war.

And all this time she was at home, home at the hotel. And was it home. In a way it was and in a way it was not, but any way it was the only home she had.

Every day and every day she had to see that everything came out from where it was put away and that everything again was put away. That was their way. That had always been their way. In that way she passed each day and each day passed away which was a night, too.

Anybody knows that a night is not a day.

She cried when she tried but even as a day was a day it came to be that way. But it was never only a day. Every day had a day in its way.

In every day there was a day in the way and it came that the day was all day.

In this way one day she tried to find the night beside and when she tried to find the night beside she cried. And her husband came home from the war and there were four children.

Now that he had come back from the war they grew richer and richer. Nothing changed but that. After a war is over if they come back from the war and they grow richer and richer sometimes everything changes and sometimes nothing changes but that.

She had come from poor people and he had not. She was very gracious and smiled sweetly and every day everything was taken out and every day everything was put away and sometimes several times during every day.

He was the cook and hotel keeper he was very busy every day.

That is the way to see a thing, see it from the outside. That makes it clear that nobody is dead yet.

They grew richer and richer every day. That was the only change every day. And every day the change was in that way. They grew richer and richer every day.

As I said they never went out and they never went away and they stayed that way.

One day he did not go away, but what happened. He was unfaithful to her. He never went away she never went away and she knew that the night was a day. Just think of it. She knew that the night was a day.

Everybody knows in a way the difference between the night and the day.

She tried to be while she cried. Oh dear yes. She tried and once when she tried, do you remember once when she tried she cried.

Lizzie, do you understand?

Everything passed away except that they did get richer every day.

That was all five years ago or so.

And now nothing happened. They were just as rich if only not richer.

The oldest boy was to be a lawyer and the second boy was to be with his father, he was to be with his mother and his father. What happened. What often does happen. He was not well and then he was to die. He is not dead. He did not die. But what happened instead. A terrible thing happened instead. A terrible thing happened instead. Somebody had to be dead. The grandmother perhaps but that was no matter.

And then everybody knew that it was true. She the mother fell out of a window onto the cement floor and then knew no more than anybody what had happened before.

She was dead then five days after and everybody said that she walked in her sleep. Did she walk in her sleep. Had she walked in her sleep. Who had walked in her sleep. Where did she walk. And whose was it that she walked. Whose was it. Can anybody cry.

Lizzie, do you mind.

1936

BUTTER WILL MELT

Once upon a time there was a chinaman. There are always many chinamen, always have been, and there are many hindoos too and there is something that is called a Hindoo chinaman and once upon a time there was one a hindoo chinaman. He had a mother and she wrote letters to him and anybody knowing the language could read them but any one not knowing the language could not read them although they were written with the letters than any frenchman or any American uses. The hindoo chinaman's name was Lien. He was not afraid of anything not even of drinking and he often was drunk and when he was he worked just the same but he was very drunk.

That made no difference because he could cook and anyway anybody who can cook is sooner or later going to take to drinking, otherwise butter would not melt.

And so he was drunk. Nobody had to be afraid of him and nobody was even when everybody was alone with him and everybody was.

Anybody is more afraid of a chinaman than of a Hindoo and Lien was a hindoo chinaman.

He was married to a hindoo chinawoman and he had children and then he was in love with a frenchwoman but he could not marry her because he was already married.

When he cooked butter did melt and so he went on cooking and he began drinking and he forgot about both of these women. His mother still was writing letters to him.

He lived in a little hotel alone and he went on cooking and drinking, which he did very well.

It was nice when he came and he said butter will melt and when he said it he did it and that made everything. That is what cooking is and cooking if the stove is always hot leads to drinking.

And so Lien kept on cooking and in between he liked to stop and go bicycling and look at anything that was to be seen. The only friend he had was a chinaman a hindoo chinaman who was more chinaman than hindoo and who was very old not to have gone back where he came from. He had a wife there too and some children but nobody wrote to him. He never could do anything butter never did melt for him and he had a little tuft of hair on his chin and he could not write or say anything and he lived very comfortably and he was not blind but everybody treated him as if he was a blind man. Lien came with him and went with him and then for a long time he never saw him again.

There was another hindo chinaman and he was young and was going to die soon and Lien hated and had hated him because they had been together once and Lien had hated him. Lien did not hate any one no hindoo chinaman can because they never see the other one again. That is what a hindoo chinaman can never do he can never hate any one because he can always go somewhere where he has not been and can come back again.

So then they have no wives and they have no children and Lien had none. His mother had had one but he had none. And then his mother did not have any children.

And so Lien never became an old man. No hindoo chinaman can, they can have consumption and then they are put in the coffin and that is the end of any hindoo chinaman.

Lien is still living and cooking and drinking and butter does melt in any pan.

1936

THE AUTOBIOGRAPHY OF ROSE

How does she know her name is Rose. She knows her name is Rose because they call her Rose. If they did not call her Rose would her name be Rose. Oh yes she knows her name is Rose.

That is the autobiography of Rose.

THE AUTOBIOGRAPHY OF ROSE.

Rose knew about afraid and when it happend she knew about afraid. This is what happened.

Grass that is cut is hay.

There there is sunshine

Here there is snow

There there is a little boy

Here there is a little girl

There his name is Allan

Here her name is Rose

It is interesting.

Rose has an autobiography even if her name was not Rose.

Let us make believe that her name is not Rose. And if her name is not Rose what would be her autobiography. It would not be the autobiography of Rose because her name would not be Rose. But it is the autobiography of Rose even if her name is not Rose oh yes indeed it is the autobiography of Rose.

THE AUTOBIOGRAPHY OF ROSE.

What happened.

Hay is grass when it is cut.

Hay has nothing to do with water.

Marshes have to do with water but not hay.

But when hay is on a hill-side and there is water. Hay can damn the water. And Rose, Rose with her father and her mother can be caught by all that water but Rose and her mother and her father were caught by all that water. That is the water went away.

THE AUTOBIOGRAPHY OF ROSE.

Nobody did not remember that her name was Rose. And if her name was Rose did that have anything to do with playing checkers and being beaten by her grandmother, oh no that had nothing to do

39

with her name being Rose.

Rose does know the difference between summer and winter and this has something to do with her name being Rose. It has something to do with her name being Rose.

THE AUTOBIOGRAPHY OF ROSE.

Rose could look at herself and when she saw herself and she knew her name was Rose she could look at herself and not see that her name is Rose. Oh yes she could. She could see that perhaps her name was not Rose.

If Rose was her name was Rose her nature.

She did not know the difference between Rose and Rose at least she said she did not know the difference between Rose and Rose.

Nobody said.

Nobody does not make any difference in her name not being Rose.

Rose is her name that is what she said.

THE AUTOBIOGRAPHY OF ROSE.

It is taller to be taller.

Is it older to be older.

Is it younger to be younger.

Is it older to be older.

Is it taller to be taller.

THE AUTOBIOGRAPHY OF ROSE.

A glass pen oh yes a glass pen.

Would Rose prefer a little dog named Pépé or a glass pen. A glass pen does not write very well and a little dog named Pépé does not allow himself to be caressed very well, so after all there is no choice there is no choice between a little dog named Pépé and a glass pen there is no choice for Rose because neither one she has not been offered either oh no she has not been offered either one.

The autobiography of Rose who has not been offered either one. If she has not been offered either one what is her autobiography. Her autobiography is not that she has not been offered either one. Indeed not. Even if she has not.

And now everybody prepare.

Rose is to be offered one.

Which one.

Which one is Rose to be offered the glass pen or a little dog named Pépé. Which one. This one. And which is this one. Ah which is this one. That is the autobiography of Rose, which is this one.

THE AUTOBIOGRAPHY OF ROSE.

When Rose was young she is young now but when Rose was young. How young does Rose have to be to be young. She was young she is young, she was very young she is young enough to be young. How young do you have to be to be young. Seven years is very young, and she knows all about being young enough to be old for a dog but not old for Rose. Seven is not old for Rose but is it young.

The autobiography of Rose is that she was young. And when she was young oh yes when she was young she said she had been young and that is quite certain she had been young. Was she regretting that she had been young so young, was she regretting anything. If she was regretting anything she was not young, how young can you be to be young. Every time Rose was young she was young. Every time and every time was every time. And now. Every time is every time. And Rose is young. Has Rose an autobiography. Rose has an autobiography. Has she an autobiography of when she was young. Rose has an autobiography of when she was young.

A garden and a gardener are two things to Rose.

And then one thing follows another.

A school succeeds a garden.

And a garden succeeds a school.

And later later succeeds a garden.

Later never sounds younger.

Oh no oh dear no

Later never sounds younger.

Older as yet.

There is no older and no as yet.

And so there is no older as yet.

Therefore older does not follow later. And not as yet.

THE AUTOBIOGRAPHY OF ROSE.

Outside now there is no Rose although in winter yes in winter often in winter quite as often as in winter there is a Rose. And as autumn does not follow winter, autumn comes first and as spring

41

very often does not follow autumn winter comes first and as summer very often comes after what is the matter with Rose knowing
it most. She does know it most. That is the autobiography of Rose
not that she knows it the most. If she knew the difference between
summer and winer and spring and autumn she would know it at
first, which she most often does and which she much the most often
does. Generally not.

Rose has only one autobiography.

This is the autobiography of Rose.

Any little while she does not neglect being taller not older. Any
little while she does not neglect. Being taller. Not older.

THE AUTOBIOGRAPHY OF ROSE.

Rose. What can she remember. Can she remember Rose. Can
she. I am wondering.

To Rose. *When they said if she would be good, she
said she would know all about it all the same, and all the
same she can know all about it. Which is a pleasure to
her friend,* Gertrude Stein.

1937

IDA

CHAPTER I

Ida is her name.

She was thinking about it she was thinking about life. She knew it was just like that through and through.

She never did want to leave it.

She did not stop thinking about it thinking about life so that is what she was thinking about. She was thinking about how she was feeling and what the people all over everywhere on the earth were doing. How could she not think about it when every day she knew what she was feeling at least she thought she did and every day she knew what everybody everywhere was doing, anyway they told her she did and she did.

You might as well just as well call her Bessie as call her Ida and if nobody likes that you might call her Emily. Perhaps Henrietta might be better because you can say Henrietta wont let her. But now let's be serious as ever is and her name is Ida, dear Ida. Somebody says that she is dead now and adored and loves everybody and somebody else likes to have it said again, dear Ida.

She always had done she always did what her husband had said she should do and then she did, well she did do what her son said she should do, but she was best of all all day either in her bed that is when she was tired or not. Please be careful not to wake her up although she mostly is awake. She does waste some time in sleep but not really. It is easy to be half awake and half asleep and to say yes I love you you do look very grand.

Now long ago Ida was like that and everybody mentioned it, dear Ida.

There is no use in Ida remembering Ernest no use at all because Ernest will always come in and stand there there where Ida has a chair even when Ida is in and out. Ida complains that all that is to come and to go. Ida is named Ida, dear Ida.

Now we are serious and circumstantial and this is the way.

Ida knew, everybody knows that they like it of course they like it if they did not it just would not go on and it does go on so what else can they do. Of course sometimes he wont let her and sometimes she wont let him and that is what life is and once in a while nobody will let anybody and then well then Ida says no no, yes I will, yes I will Ida says and she says yes and then they begin again. What do they begin. They begin going on not letting anybody do anything and by that time Ida is rested of course she is. She is rested but she thinks her son might be more careful and pretty soon he is and everybody is more careful. And then pretty soon everybody is forgetting and forgot nice Ida.

<h2 style="text-align:center">CHAPTER III</h2>

Like all who are on a boat Ida is on land, now there are three things there is up in the air.

Ida lived through it all not that she ever did it, she did nothing, she neither waited nor refused, how busy she was doing neither the one or the other, how busy she was.

It could make anybody cry to think how busy she was, and she was busy very very busy.

And then well then the question came should you do what they tell you or should you not.

Who tells you what to do. Well somebody always tells somebody what to do. That is what life is. Believe it or not they do they do tell you what to do.

Policemen are like that they just hold up their hand.

Like everything Ida thinks about she thinks about that.

She thinks everybody will be a policeman by and by even you and I.

Not that she will, not that I will. Ida will not she will not be a policeman she has to rest and a policeman has a vacation but he never takes a rest.

Dear Ida, sweet Ida, Ida, Ida.

<h2 style="text-align:center">CHAPTER IV</h2>

Once upon a time Ida had a father and a mother. Once upon a time she had a husband and a stepfather, once upon a time she had a brother and a cousin once upon a time she had two sets of children.

Dear Ida.

But really what was Ida.

CHAPTER V

Ida used to sit and as she sat she said am I one or am I two. Little by little she was one of two, that is to say sometimes she went out as one and sometimes she went out as the other.

Everybody got confused they did not know which was which but Ida did, whichever one she was she had always to think about what life was and what was it.

Well now just what was it.

When she was one that is when she was not the other one, everybody admired her, she even had a beauty prize for being the most beautiful one, when she was the other one she had a prize too she had a prize for not remembering any one or anything.

That is not the same as a beauty prize, no policeman and no beauty can have that prize, the prize for not remembering anything or any one.

And so Ida dear Ida had everything she even had two sets of children and two husbands, the first one died before the other one, he was really dead, you see Ida did have everything.

Dear Ida.

CHAPTER VI

And now comes the really exciting moment in the life of Ida. She had it to tell and she did tell it and every one wanted it. Oh yes they did.

Ida was no longer two she was one and she had every one.

Everybody knew about her.

Oh yes they did.

And why

Ida was her name

That was her fame.

Ida was her name.

Oh yes it was.

That is the way it comes about.

After that everybody knew just who Ida was where she came from and what happened.

It did happen.

Everybody knew her name.

And Ida was her name.

It was an exciting time.

That was what happened to Ida.

Nobody said dear Ida any more they just said Ida and when they said Ida everybody knew it was Ida.

Alas nobody cried when they said it was Ida.

She knew, she knew that five is more than ten she knew that six is more than eight, she knew the weight, the real weight of the slate it was a large slate upon which she wrote, she did not really write but on the slate there it was, it was Ida.

Anybody can happen to be there and Ida was always there.

All who knew better than that knew better than to be fat.

Now let us make it all careful and clear.

Everybody is an Ida.

Dear Ida.

Everybody hears everybody when they are heard but that might mean that there is a third but there is not there is only Ida.

Don't all cry although you might all have a try yes you might, you might all have a try just as well as Ida.

It is just as easy to please.

Now Ida never pleased she never had to they were all pleased.

Just like that they were all pleased, oh yes why not, it was Ida, yes it was.

CHAPTER VII

And so from the beginning and there was no end there was Ida.

Think of any advertisement, think of anything to eat, there was only Ida.

Dear brave Ida.

Anybody can see that it was all stored all the love of Ida.

Stored and adored.

Bored and reward

All for love of Ida.

Not that they loved Ida.

Nobody does that but they did know and Ida told them so that it was so. Of course it was so. Dear Ida.

So you see now again they say dear Ida.

Don't you see how it all happened.

Of course it does happen.

But you do see how it will happen.

It will always happen.

Nobody neglects anything.

There is always that, he says she says, there is always that.

46

Dear Ida.

Once more dear Ida.

I wonder if you understand about that if you did well if you did remember me to Ida. Dear Ida.

1937

IX
Questions and Answers

As a well known creative artist, Gertrude Stein was frequently asked for statements of her opinion about the arts or the state of the arts in her time. Answering she usually regarded as a sport or a warm up for a statement she'd always wanted to make. In later life Gertrude Stein regarded questions as the province of the sciences, and found them irrelevant in the arts. Her famous deathbed scene confirms this: "What is the answer? . . . In that case, what is the question?" The implication is if any. Certainly there was a scientific question and a scientific answer; she was dying. But once that was established, there was only the "other realm." In that realm, as in the realm of aesthetics, where she had always lived and worked, there was only the thing created, the life fulfilled.

"Why I Do Not Live in America" was prepared for transition *in the Fall of 1928. Not yet an international figure, Gertrude Stein brushes aside the specific questions to answer with a brief credo about the need for two cultures. She is optimistic about the past and the future of America. Her present is Paris, individualism and "thinking in writing."*

"Answers to Jane Heap" was published in the Little Review, *May 1929. To a very silly questionnaire she gives apparently silly answers, but they reveal a gratified person, with a strong sense of ego and self-preservation, and very comfortable in her world.*

"Answer to Eugene Jolas" appeared in transition, March 1933. *In response to Jolas' rather elaborate and overblown statement, Gertrude Stein assumes her most deliberately homespun stance. She votes for individualism. It is her apple-pie. This is the writer whose* Autobiography of Alice B. Toklas *(1933) was about to become a best-seller and catapult her into international recognition. tion.*

"Answers to the Partisan Review*" appeared in that magazine in the summer of 1939. This is Gertrude Stein on the eve of the European war—politically out of touch but personally sure of her philosophy and her vocation. She is still committed to the present. Criticism being "too late" is not interesting. The audience is flattering and agreeable but not to be mixed into the business of writing. Compared with "Why I Do Not Live in America," this is a more fully thought through writer's statement. The interval between was a decade.*

WHY I DO NOT LIVE IN AMERICA

WHY DO AMERICANS LIVE IN EUROPE?

Transition *has asked a number of Americans living in Europe to write brief stories of themselves—their autobiographies of the mind, self-examinations, confessions, conceived from the standpoint of deracination.*
The following questions were asked:
1. Why do you prefer to live outside America?
2. How do you envisage the spiritual future of America in the face of a dying Europe and in the face of a Russia that is adopting the American economic vision?
3. What is your feeling about the revolutionary spirit of your age as expressed, for instance, in such movements as communism, surrealism, anarchism?
4. What particular vision do you have of yourself in relation to twentieth century reality?

WHY I DO NOT LIVE IN AMERICA

The United States is just now the oldest country in the world, there always is an oldest country and she is it, it is she who is the mother of the twentieth century civilisation. She began to feel herself as it just after the Civil War. And so it is a country the right age to have been born in and the wrong age to live in.

She is the mother of modern civilisation and one wants to have been born in the country that has attained and live in the countries that are attaining or going to be attaining. This is perfectly natural if you only look at facts as they are. America is now early Victorian very early Victorian, she is a rich and well nourished home but not a place to work. Your parent's home is never a place to work it is a nice place to be brought up in. Later on there will be place enough to get away from home in the United States, it is beginning, then there will be creators who live at home. A country this is the oldest and therefore the most important country in the world quite naturally produces the creators, and so naturally it is I an American who was and is thinking in writing was born in America and live in Paris. This has been and probably will be the history of the world. That it is always going to be like that makes the monotony and variety of life that and that we are after all all of us ourselves.

1928

ANSWERS TO JANE HEAP

1. *What should you most like to do, to know, to be? (In case you are not satisfied.)*
2. *Why wouldn't you change places with any other human being?*
3. *What do you look forward to?*
4. *What do you fear most from the future?*
5. *What has been the happiest moment of your life? The unhappiest? (If you care to tell.)*
6. *What do you consider your weakest characteristics? Your strongest? What do you like most about yourself? -Dislike most?*
7. *What things do you really like? Dislike? (Nature, people, ideas, objects, etc. Answer in a phrase or a page, as you will.)*
8. *What is your attitude toward art today?*
9. *What is your world view? (Are you a reasonable being in a reasonable scheme?)*
10. *Why do you go on living?*

ANSWERS TO JANE HEAP

Good luck to your last number. I would much rather have written about Jane because I do appreciate Jane but since this is what you want here are my answers.

1. But I am.
2. Because I am I.
3. More of the same.
4. Anything.
5. Birthday.
6. 1. Weakness. 2. Nothing. 3. Everything. 4. Almost anything.
7. 1. What I like. 2. Hardly anything.
8. I like to look at it.
9. Not very likely or often.
10. I am.

1929

ANSWER TO EUGENE JOLAS

The crisis through which we are passing today is primarily a crisis of human consciousness.

The post-war disquietude still continues into the present epoch. But whereas up till recently, this chaos was celebrated as an inescapable state of affairs, we find today a strong current towards some sort of spiritual renovation.

Man's consciousness is going through a crisis, because the age seems to tend in the direction of social grouping as a result of economic necessity. The intellectual atmosphere produced by this gregarious hypnosis threatens to make a man a mere number in a collectivity.

I believe that the individual is about to revolt. The human personality long suppressed by the machine is ready to rebel against the uniformisation which grimaces in the offing.

In the following pages I present professions of faith by a number of European and American writers and scientists regarding the evolution of individualism and metaphysics under a collectivistic regime.

Eugene Jolas

ANSWER TO EUGENE JOLAS

I don't envisage collectivism. There is no such animal, it is always individualism, sometimes the rest vote and sometimes they do not, and if they do they do and if they do not they do not.

1933

ANSWERS TO THE *PARTISAN REVIEW*

THE SITUATION IN AMERICAN WRITING

1. *Are you conscious, in your own writing, of the existence of a "usable past"? Is this mostly American? What figures would you designate as elements in it? Would you say, for example, that Henry James's work is more relevant to the present and future of American writing than Walt Whitman's?*

2. *Do you think of yourself as writing for a definite audience? If so, how would you describe this audience? Would you say that the audience for serious American writing has grown or contracted in the last ten years?*

3. *Do you place much value on the criticism your work has received? Would you agree that the corruption of the literary supplements—by advertising—in the case of the newspapers —and political pressures—in the case of the liberal weeklies —has made serious literary criticism an isolated cult?*

4. *Have you found it possible to make a living by writing the sort of thing you want to, and without the aid of such crutches as teaching and editorial work? Do you think there is any place in our present economic system for literature as a profession?*

5. *Do you find, in retrospect, that your writing reveals any allegiance to any group, class, organization, region, religion, or system of thought, or do you conceive of it as mainly the expression of yourself as an individual?*

6. *How would you describe the political tendency of American writing as a whole since 1930? How do you feel about it yourself? Are you sympathetic to the current tendency towards what may be called "literary nationalism"—a renewed emphasis, largely uncritical, on the specifically "American" elements in our culture?*

7. *Have you considered the question of your attitude towards the possible entry of the United States into the next world war? What do you think the responsibilities of writers in general are when and if war comes?*

I am afraid the questions are not the kind that interest me a lot but I have written down an answer to each one anyway.

1.   Usable for what, cannot worry about the future of American writing, the present is enough, and any American is American.

2.   An audience is pleasant if you have it, it is flattering and flattering is agreeable always, but if you have an audience the being an audience is their business, they are the audience you are the writer, let each attend to their own business.

3.   After all if it is written and presumably what you write is written before it is criticised then criticism is bound to come too late always. To the rest of the question it is the same.

4.   I suppose if I had had to make a living I should have, I do not know, how can you tell.

5.   I am not interested.

6.   Writers only think they are interested in politics, they are not really, it gives them a chance to talk and writers like to talk but really no real writer is really interested in politics.

7.   It does not seem possible for any of you to realise that most probably there will not be another general European war, the more America thinks there is going to be one the more suspicious the continent gets and the less likely they are to fight. Anyway they are not at all likely to do so but if they were to then the writers would have to fight too like anybody else, some will like it and some will not.

1939

X
Identity

From 1933, the date of the appearance of The Autobiography of Alice B. Toklas, *to 1945, the year of Gertrude Stein's death, she was a celebrity. She suffered her particular "identity crisis" when she discovered that the character of her writing had been affected by the consciousness of an audience. "An audience is pleasant if you have it," she had written, "it is flattering and flattering is agreeable always . . ." Audience writing, for her, was serving Mammon rather than God. The volume of such writing increased in her last decade because tantalizing offers to print her work flowed in.* The Autobiography of Alice B. Toklas *(1933),* Lectures in America *(1934),* Narration *(1935),* What Are Masterpieces *(1935),* Everybody's Autobiography *(1936),* Paris France *(1939),* Wars I Have Seen *(1942) and all of the pieces in this section of the Uncollected Writings come under the rubric of being written for popular consumption, or with an audience in mind.*

The charm and wit and wisdom, the ease and flow and individuality of these last works are appealing. If some of the pioneering fight of her earlier, lonelier days of working with words was gone, she had nevertheless come to terms with her medium of expression, and the American language of today moves in new ways because of her.

The following groups represent areas of concern for her in this last phase.

AUTOBIOGRAPHY:

"The Story of a Book" ultimately became a part of Everybody's Autobiography *(1936). It describes how Gertrude Stein first discovered she had a public.*

"And Now" tells something about Gertrude Stein's "identity crisis" ("When the success began and it was a success I got completely lost.") and about her slow recovery from it prior to the American lecture tour of 1934/1935.

AMERICA:

This series was written for the New York Herald Tribune. *They are improvisations on various unique themes.*

"I Came and Here I Am" reflects Gertrude Stein's thoughts about returning to her native land after an absence of over thirty years, and her first experiences of New York, of flying, of radio-broadcasting and American football. When this article was published by the Cosmopolitan, *the editors punctuated it to make it more "comprehensible" for their readers. The whereabouts of the manuscript is presently unknown, and we are unable to restore Gertrude Stein's text as written.*

"The Capital and Capitals of the United States of America"—a meditation on why Americans are both friendly and suspicious and why practically no state has its capital in its biggest city.

"American States and Cities and How They Differ From Each Other" traces Gertrude Stein's feeling for the uniqueness of American states, towns and inhabitants. Her extensive lecture tour rekindled ideas she had written in Useful Knowledge *(1928).*

"American Food and American Houses" describes American food as moist and French food as not. Gertrude Stein lovingly contrasts the cuisines of both countries, as well as the differences in family living. In this series of essays we see how and in what detail Alice Toklas and Gertrude Stein reexplored America.

"American Education and American Colleges" tells us that "Very likely education does not make very much difference—" even though the educators who do it like it.

"American Crimes and How They Matter" turns upon the idea that there are "two kinds of crime that help the imagination, the crime hero and the crime mystery, all other crimes everybody forgets as soon as they find out who did them." Dillinger, Baby-Face, Hauptmann, Mill and Lizzie Borden come in for comment.

MONEY:

This series was written by Gertrude Stein for the Saturday Evening Post. *Each new issue was a surprise and a matter of amusement for everyday readers of the magazine. They contain a kind of authority and mother-wit which holds the attention for a short space of time, much as a political cartoon might. I remember going into several homes, at the time, where the* Post *had been folded open to the Gertrude Stein page and left conspicuously on a table to attract notice. It is a little difficult today to understand why, in those post-depression Rooseveltian years, such a ringing of changes on private money and public spending, individual fredom and governmental organization was refreshing. But it was.*

WORLD WAR II:

Four pieces about Gertrude Stein's experience in World War II France where she preferred to live out her life during the war itself and after. There is a picture of country life in occupied France, of liberation day, of the return to Paris and the famous apartment and collection, of the trip into Germany with the American army, and a comparison of the "lost generation" of World War I with the soldiers returning home from World War II.

READING, WRITING AND SPEAKING:

"Why I like Detective Stories" is based on Gertrude Stein's avid passion for reading them. The original version of the "Prothalamium" was written on the fly leaf of an Edgar Wallace. An interesting phenomenon is the appearance of an imaginary interior dialogue between Edgar Wallace and his chief auxiliary-ego, Edgar II. Today this is a recognized therapeutic device. We learn that "Blood on the Dining Room Floor" had no corpses but some generalized detecting, and that "A Piano and A Waterfall" and "Is Dead" had corpses but no detecting. Gertrude Stein's wish was to innovate by creating a detective story with no motive and no detecting. This is another example of how systematically she thought about her literary options—such as can detective stories produce any other effect than either being soothing or frightening? If there was something else, Gertrude Stein wanted to do it.

"How Writing is Written": a summary statement on the artist's responsibility to live life in the present and to express himself contemporaneously, and to express things "as a whole" in the Twentieth Century, rather than "built up out of its parts" as in the Nineteenth. Gertrude Stein traces her literary development from The Making of Americans *to* Four Saints *and makes clear her life-long commitment to "present immediacy" in writing.*

60

THE STORY OF A BOOK

If there had not been a beautiful and unusual dry October at Bilignin in France in 1932 followed by an unusually dry and beautiful first two weeks of November would the autobiography of Alice B. Toklas have been written? Possibly but probably not then.

Every day during those beautiful six weeks of unusually dry and sunny days, in the morning and in the afternoon, I sat and on a little double decked table as near the sunny wall as I could get I wrote about five hours a day. This is a very unusual thing for me to do because although I always write I do not write very long at a time but I wrote without excitement and steadily and in six weeks the autobiography was done.

I did not write to anybody about the autobiography, I usually do write to anybody I write to, about what I am doing, but only to Bernard Fay and Bromfield I mentioned that I was doing something and perhaps it might be interesting.

When it was all done I said to Alice B. Toklas, do you think it is going to be a best seller, I would love to write a best seller. She said, wait until I typewrite it and then I will tell you.

She typed it but she did not tell me whether it was a best seller but we were pleased and so I wrote to my literary agent, Mr. Bradley in Paris, and told him I was sending him the first half of a manuscript which might interest him. He had always been interested in my manuscripts but, to his and my regret, had had only with them what the French call a succès d'estime, in other words they had not been best sellers.

To my delight, the day after he received the first half of the manuscript he telegraphed me a long telegram impatiently demanding the second half and promising me a conspicuous succès d'estime and commercial as well. I was pleased.

The manuscript was then sent to the publishers we selected and to *The Atlantic Monthly*. The letters and cables of enthusiasm were such as Mr. Bradley says he has never received in all his experience. Needless to say I who have as an author hitherto never aroused any enthusiasm in any publisher except the publisher of *Plain Edition*, Alice B. Toklas, was naturally overwhelmed. This was crowned by the letter of Mr. Aswell of the *Atlantic Monthly* who described as follows his experience with the manuscript:

"Your manuscript met with such an unusual reception in our office that I think I ought to tell you about it. Mr. Bradley addressed the manuscript to me, and sent with it a myserious letter in which he refused to divulge the identity of the author other than to say that she was a well-known American writer living in Paris. I opened the package about ten o'clock of a very dull morning, rather annoyed by what I took to be a trick of Mr. Bradley's to pique my curiosity, and vastly bored by the prospect of having to wade through so many reams of anonymous wood-pulp. (An editor, who has to digest a thousand pages of drivel for every page he prints, soon falls into a state of chronic boredom from which only the exceptional manuscript can release him.)

"In this state of mind I settled down to *Toklas*. I read the first pages and right there you had me. I was instantly fascinated and went on reading, turning page after page automatically, not knowing that I turned them, so completely absorbed had I become in your story. At last I was recalled to awareness of the here and now by an increasing darkness in the room. There was hardly light enough for me to see the page before me. I thought a storm had come up and glanced out the window. There were no clouds, but the sky looked quer. I pulled out my watch. It was after five o'clock and the sun was setting! I could not believe it, but it was so. I had forgotten time, forgotten my lunch, forgotten a dozen things I had meant to do that day, so entirely had I been caught by the spell of your words. I rushed at once to Mr. Sedgwick and told him about it. 'Such a thing never happened before in this office,' he exclaimed, and he was right—it never had.

"So we accepted the manuscript and now it is about to be published. If you could do this to an editor, of all people the least susceptible to the magic of print, what I wonder, will be the effect of your story on the general public?"

It can easily be realized that after these years of faith that there is and was a public and that somtime I would come in contact with that public, as I said in *The Making of Americans* which I wrote twenty-seven years ago, I write for myself and strangers, after these years to know that I have a public gives me what the French call a coeur léger, it makes me not light-hearted but it leaves me unburdened.

And the readers of the autobiography will not only read the autobiography but they will read and see everything that has made the autobiography. And so all this which has pleased and contented me will please and content them.

1933

AND NOW

The other book was gay, this one will not be so gay. The other had peace and war. This one has peace and only peace and so it is not going to be so gay. It is going to be rather sad. When there has been a long peace after there has been a long war, there is a monotone and something of a moan. That is where we are to-day. There is a great deal to say about where we are to-day and what is happening every day.

What happened from the day I wrote the autobiography to to-day and what do I think about it all, about what happened every day.

I make my bow.

I have always quarreled with a great many young men and one of the principal things that I have quarreled with them about was that once they had made a success they became sterile, they could not go on. And I blamed them. I said it was their fault. I said success is all right but if there is anything in you it ought not to cut off the flow not if there is anything in you. Now I know better. It does cut off your flow and then if you are not too young and you are frightened enough you can begin again but if you are young or if you were young when you succeeded then when you get frightened it makes it worse not better.

That is the advantage of being older when you get frightened it starts you going, when you are young and you get frightened it just stops you more than ever. Just think of animals and children and you will understand.

What happened to me was this. When the success began and it was a success I got lost completely lost. You know the nursery rhyme, I am I because my little dog knows me. Well you see I did not know myself, I lost my personality. It has always been completely included in myself my personality as any personality naturally is, and here all of a sudden, I was not just I because so many people did know me. It was just the opposite of I am I because my little dog knows me. So many people knowing me I was I no longer and for the first time since I had begun to write I could not write and what was worse I could not worry about not writing and what was also worse I began to think about how my writing would sound to others, how could I make them understand, I who had always lived within myself and my writing. And then all of a sudden

63

I said there that it is that is what was the matter with all of them all the young men whose syrup did not pour, and here I am being just the same. They were young and I am not but when it happens it is just the same, the syrup does not pour.

It did not frighten me, I was enjoying myself. I was spending my money as they had spent their money all the other painters and writers that I had blamed and condemned and here I was doing the same thing. And then the dollar fell and somehow I got frightened, really frightened awfully frightened just as all of them had gotten frightened really frightened these last years, but luckily for me being older the fright has made me write. I say luckily for me because I like to write. It is what I like best. I like it even better than spending money although there is no pleasure so sweet as the pleasure of spending money but the pleasure of writing is longer. There is no denying that.

All this is to introduce what happened since the writing of the autobiography and a great many things have happened.

In the first place Picasso and I are no longer friends. All the writers about whom I wrote wrote to me that they liked what I wrote but none of the painters. The painters did not like what I wrote about them, they none of them did. They just as Henry McBride afterward told me that Matisse did, they shuddered.

I remember when there was the first big show at the autumn salon, I imagine about 1905, of Cézanne, his really first serious public recognition, they told the story that he was so moved he said he would now have to paint more carefully than ever. And then he painted those last pictures of his that were more than ever covered over painted and painted over. Perhaps it is like that.

But to tell it all just as it had happened because of course a great deal has happened not only to me and to everybody I knew but to everything else. Once more Paris is not as it was.

When Picabia came to see us in the country he told me that there had been three young Spaniards who showed their pictures in 1904 and 1905 at a small furniture shop at Montmartre. The other two were Picasso and the unknown, the one who did the café and the one everybody has forgotten, and the third was himself Picabia. They were to have another show together the following winter but by that time Picasso and we had discovered each other and they did not have their show together. This is what Picabia told me and I was very surprised as at that time I never heard of Picabia.

When he was younger and young Picabia was very Spanish or rather very Cuban. He had the rather boring quality of the Cubans

64

that mixture that one finds also in the South Americans of the old civilization that has not become new and the new civilization that never becomes new. Therein very different from Northern America which is all new, the old gets lost before it becomes new because the new is always becoming new.

Picabia now had lost a great deal of the Cuban. His grandfather was of course extremely French. He told us a nice story the other day. He never sees his French cousins any more although he has quantities of them but they all, he and the French cousins, do from time to time go to see the old concierges, janitors, Alsatians, who were caretakers for his grandfather and they ask the news about each other, and what, said they all to the concierge, is Picabia like now, they were all interested because he had just been given the legion of honor and a picture of his had just been accepted by the Luxembourg, and what, said Picabia to the concierge, did you answer when they asked you. Why I said exactly like his grandfather. And that is the true story of something that has been important in painting.

There was another funny photographic link. In those early days a photographer came to Paris and knew us all. He was Steichen. He had been one of Steiglitz' men and came over very excited about photography. Pretty soon he decided that ordinary painting did not interest him, one could do all that with photography, that is to say that the photographs of pictures looked just like the photographs of real landscapes or of still lives if they were good pictures, and so there must be something else and so he became very interested in modern painting and was one of those who told Steiglitz and the rest of them all about it.

One other funny thing happened at that time that I had forgotten all about and was reminded by a very nice letter from Lee Simonson. In those early days Simonson very young and very New York came to Paris. At Harvard he had been defending Monet and he came to Paris intending to carry on the crusade. He came to a Paris where there was no Monet to defend. Of course there was no Monet to defend. He was very upset by this but we all liked him because he told it to us.

Another thing in a little later than these days, in fact just after the war. Janet Scudder was getting tired of sculpure, she wanted to be a painter and paint. She said she always had wanted to be a painter and now the time had come. So she painted some pictures and wanted to send them to the new spring salon. There is a rule at the salon that a member of one cannot exhibit at another and

Janet was a member of the old spring salon and so she could not exhibit at the new and she suggested to Alice B. Toklas that she Janet would exhibit under her name and Alice was amused and consented. Of course no one else was told anything about it. The picture was accepted and hung and we went over to look at it and brought home a catalogue. That evening Picasso came to the house. I showed him the catalogue. What he said, she has always painted and I never knew it. No I said she had never painted before she just painted this one picture and sent it to the salon and it was accepted. It is not possible he said angrily, it is not possible. Nobody who has never drawn or painted a picture can paint a first picture and send it to any salon and have it accepted, it is not possible. But there you are, I said. It is not possible he answered stubbornly. He was terribly upset. He said that would upset everything if it were possible. The salons may not be great painting but you have to have a technique to pass the jury and if you never painted before it is not possible. He was so upset that I began to laugh. What is the story he demanded. I told him and he was so relieved. I knew he said that it was not possible. It just could not be possible otherwise nothing would have any meaning.

Even now A. B. Toklas gets catalogues of paints sent to her faithfully by art shops in hopes that she will yet paint another picture.

But now. Paris has changed and I have changed and I am no longer frightened and I will just as well change again but at present it is all very changed.

I write the way I used to write in *The Making of Americans*, I wander around. I come home and I write, I write in one copy-book and I copy what I write into another copy-book and I write and I write. Just at present I write about American religion and Grant, Ulysses Simpson Grant, and I have come back to write the way I used to write and this is because now everything that is happening is once more happening inside, there is no use in the outside, if you see the outside you see just what you look at and that is no longer interesting, everybody says so or at least everybody acts so and they are right because now there is no use in looking at anything. If it is going to change it is of no interest and if it is not going to change it is of no interest and so what is the use of looking, everything you see is what nobody looks at and so just as so long ago everything went on inside now everything goes on inside. Incidentally, there is a new young painter and when I know more about him I will tell about him.

And so the time comes when I can tell the history of my life.

1934

I CAME AND HERE I AM

What has my life in America been, it has been the doing of everything that I never have done. Never have done, never could have done, never could have done again; that is the way my life in America began and is begun and is going on.

Before I came, before I began to come, while I was still in France, I wrote about meditating upon what would come, what would happen when I came. What will they say to me and what will I say to them, those who make in my native land my native land? I cannot believe that America has changed, many things have come and gone but not really come and not really gone, but they are there and that perhaps does make the America that I left and the America I am to find different but not really different—it would be impossible for it to be really different or for me to find that it was really different . . .

That is the way I meditated before I came and then I came and here I am.

I had not been here for thirty-one years, that is a long time; twenty-five years roll around so quickly but thirty-one years is a long time.

As a man said to me, we were buying fruit on Seventh Avenue, I know you by your picture, you are the lady who has not been here for thirty-one years. But after all it is natural enough, not the thirty-one years but the being here, it is so natural that it is not real.

No one could say, not even we, that it was just all the same. Here we were. And it was all strange and it was all natural, as natural as strange and as strange as natural.

And what was strange?

Well, the shapes of the trucks on the streets were strange, the little lights, such pretty lights on top of the taxis, they were strange, very strange. I cannot say they were natural, they were just strange. And the special highways, they were strange but they were the things that were almost natural, although they were so strange. A road, built by man to carry things that move, was natural and strange, and they differ from tunnels or subways or elevated roads, because they are not rigid, they have a life of their own and they move in that life as country roads do, only they are neither on the earth nor in the air, they were what I knew America was when I used to say what America is, only now it had been done, America had been able to do what America is. And it was very exhilarating to know that this that America was had been done to be what America is. It was most exciting.

And then it began. The doing everything that I had never done, and the liking doing everything everything anything that I had never done. That began. And this is the way it began.

You can but you cannot imagine how astonishing it was everything that was happening.

The first thing that happened was what they called a newsreel. I know it is very hard for anybody to believe and I had never thought about it but I had never seen a talking cinema, never. You see, I have as you see got into the habit of talking to anybody so I am writing as if I am talking; well, you do see that in my quiet life in Paris, where nothing much changes as one is very busy, just writing and eating and sleeping and walking and talking, I just never had seen a talking cinema, and when they said to me will you make one, it was just to me like nothing at all.

That is really all I can say about it, and so they proceeded to make one and I did just what they told me and it was not even astonishing and it certainly was not natural but they made one. Then they told me it was successful and they asked me to go to see it. And I did. It was a strange thing that happened to me. One never gets quite used to unexpectedly seeing one's name in print no matter how often it happens to you to be that one; it always gives you a shock of a slightly mixed-up feeling, are you or are you not one. No matter how often it happens there is always this thing, but what is that, imagine what is that compared to never having heard anybody's voice speaking while a picture is doing something, and that voice and that person is yourself, if you could really and truly be that one. It upset me very much when that happened to me, there is no doubt about that, if there can really not be any doubt about anything.

And then while all these things, while everything was happening, that was astonishing; there were the people and the buildings and they were the most natural and the most unreal thing of everything that was happening.

About the buildings there were two things happening. The big high buildings and how we liked to look and look at them, and the ordinary wooden houses and how we liked to look at them whenever we saw them. Old ones and new ones, dark and unpainted and white and clean ones, we liked we liked so to look at them and see them. But the high buildings, Alice B. Toklas felt very faint when she first really knew that she saw them.

But all the time there were streets and the people in them and they made everything, and I must tell you about this thing.

The streets.

They all know me and I know all of them, that is so comfortable and so comforting.

When it was first happening, it was surprising rather than astonishing, and it was not disturbing, it was pleasant, natural and comforting. Let me tell you about it.

The first evening we went out to buy an apple. We went in and the man said Good evening, Miss Stein, did you have a nice trip. That was surprising but then perhaps he did know who I was, and it was very nice of him. That is the way I felt about it, then we went on, and slowly, I realized that one after another said my name, and then someone took off his hat and said Good evening, Miss Stein. I wondered did I perhaps know him. And then suddenly and slowly I began to realize that they knew who I was. It was curious, it was pleasant, it was comforting.

One said How do you do, they stopped and looked and I looked at them, I found I could smile at anyone and they knew why I smiled at them, because I knew that they would know that I knew that they knew me and that I knew them. It was a strange sensation but such a natural one. Everybody did it. It went on all the time and it still goes on and it pleases me very much. It is just like living in the country where I live and there are very few people and where I know anybody and everybody knows me as a perfectly natural thing, and if you like, if you think about it, it is a surprising thing that the largest city in the world should have a population as gentle and pleasant and intimate and considerate and comforting as a little bit of a place where everybody knows everybody and everything, but astonishing or not it is perfectly true and the inhabitants of New York are just like that, and they are like that and this thing is a delightful, natural and gentle and sweet and comforting thing.

So there we were and the people, all the people, were there with us and the buildings were there too beside us and the lights, it is wonderful that everybody does just what the lights tell them to do, But I can understand that as the lights know so well just what they should tell, and so they and the automobiles do completely and naturally understand everything. It is very clear and very impressive, it really is, and very law-abiding which is not at all what I thought it would be from everything I had been hearing, and all the time everything was happening all day and every day, and there was lecturing and that was exciting and everything, and then we were to go to Chicago and back, and we were to fly, and once more as always we were doing what we had never done before and never would have done, and it was natural, just as natural as breathing, to do everything that we had never done. And we flew and this is what I wrote while I was flying.

Meditations in my first airplane.

In the first place airplanes were made for writers because it is so easy and so comfortable to write in them and you cannot talk and so why not write. Which I do. I like the little bumps it gives, otherwise there would be no difference between it and being at home, and the difference between it and being home is so great that it is nice that there are the little differences, just those little differences of little bumps.

Why did nobody tell me before I got on that the air is solid. Of course it is solid, it is just as solid as water. When you look out at air from a high place it is not solid but when it is all around you it is solid, and so you cannot be afraid and you have to feel perfectly comfortable and this is what I do and most astonishing too, astonishing to me but not to Carl Van Vechten who said that that would be the way it would be, only he did not tell me that the air was solid but it is; what is the difference between air and water, not very much, not when you are in an airplane and when you are in a boat, but it is, the air is just as solid as that.

I always liked boats but rocked in the cradle of the deep is nothing to being rocked in the cradle of the sky, the air is so sweetly solid and being able to go every way is so much better than just being able to go one way. The earth now, as far as I am concerned, is something that has been, and when you come back to it, it is a disappointment and the other side of the clouds is all right, you know that by its light, the light of the clouds, the white light of the clouds, and you recognize it, but you like it more than just recognizing. It is just what I imagine arctic fields to be and ever since I could read, I liked to read about arctic ice fields, and I would never have had the courage to go to the North Pole to see the ice fields but here they are with the thin light and the white light and the sunlight.

And also then there is the stewardess and the pilots and that is what makes it all so real and so unreal, she is just nice and talks United States and is helpful and friendly in the best United States

70

way, is well informed and kindly and protective and in the best United States way there is a pistol hanging low to shoot man and the sky in the best United States way, and the pistol is I know a dark steel-blue pistol.

And so I know everything I know. And now I am on my way back and I have distinctly found out what it is, what it all is; it is just like a railroad train when we crossed the continent when I was a child. It keeps straight on its tracks and just as fast as it can go straight on its tracks, and it hums just as it did then when I leaned my head near the open window and then, as it slackens its speed, it bumps gently just as the train did when it went over the ties and then, as it slows down some more, it bumps some more, just as the train did then, and it stops just as the train did then, a little roughly. The only difference is that mostly, as you look out, nothing goes by. But you soon get used to that.

So after all that is that, and that is why whether it is on the earth or in the sky it is so natural at once and by and by.

Tonight I did the last thing that I never did before. I used to say when anybody asked me to go anywhere yes I will go anywhere once. But broadcasting is not like that no it is not like that, of all things that I never did before, perhaps I like this the best.

In writing in *The Making of Americans* I said I write for myself and strangers and this is what broadcasting is. I write for myself and strangers.

It is difficult to believe but it is true, I had never heard a broadcasting; that is I had never listened to one and I certainly had never thought of doing one, and this is the way the thing that I like best of all the things I have never done before, was done. They said would I and I of course said I would. I never say no, not in America.

The first thing they did was to photograph me doing it, not doing it but making believe doing it, this was easily done. There was nothing natural or unnatural about that.

And then we went into training. I liked that; I wrote out answers to questions and questions to answers and I liked that, and then one day the day had come, and it was to be done.

We went there, there were so many rooms and all the rooms were empty rooms, that was all right; and then all of a sudden we were in a little room, and they were going to time us and they did. That seemed to me very well done, they knew so well how to do this thing and no fuss was made about anything, and then I was taken into another room and there there were more people but by that

71

time I was not noticing much of anything.

Then we sat down one on either side of the little thing that was between us and I said something and they said that is all, and then suddenly it was all going on. It was it was really all going on, and it was, it really was, as if you were saying what you were saying and you knew, you really knew, not by what you knew but by what you felt, that everybody was listening. It is a very wonderful thing to do, I almost stopped and said it, I was so filled with it. And then it was over and I never had liked anything as I had liked it.

This then was the last completion, of what is, that is that the unreal is natural, so natural that it makes of unreality the most natural of anything natural. That is what America does, and that is what America is. Long ago, oh way long ago, long before I had ever dreamed of these things that prove it, I said, that what made America and American literature was a quality of being disembodied, and I said there was Emerson, and there was Hawthorne and there was Edgar Poe and there was Walt Whitman and there was, well, in a funny way, there was Mark Twain and then there was Henry James and then there was—well, there is—well, I am. So you see one follows the other and they are all, well, they are all abstract, if you know what I mean, and the color is, and the land is, and the buildings are, and everything is, and so and so the red Indian was, and is.

When I was taken to New Haven to see Dartmouth beaten, Dartmouth was beautiful while it was being beaten; I said what there was about it that was so interesting was that it was an American thing, not football anybody's football, but the way, the American way, that they were doing that thing. It was like Indian dancing. And that is natural enough because the soil makes the way anybody is moving, and they and the Indians had been and were being, made by the same thing.

They, in the Indian way, they put their heads down and in a circle there they stay. And then the substitutes do the little Indian movement just the way the Indians do any day. And then and that is the most so they come down on all fours, anybody knows that is just just the way the Indian does it any day. And then they all look at the big brown ball.

It is a real Indian dance, and before they were so American, as they are now, they did not do it in that way, they did not do football in that way.

And that is what America is, is and is and it is beautiful, beautiful in the American way, beautiful just in this way.

1935

72

THE CAPITAL AND CAPITALS OF THE UNITED STATES OF AMERICA

There are a great many strange things that are or are not strange here in America and perhaps the strangest is where the capital of the country is that is where the capitals of the country are.

The capitals of important countries are in the big important city of the important country. That is always true. The important big city of an important country is always its capital.

But not in America and does anybody know except by history as to why this is so. But history is not an explanation there is a reason behind and this is what I want to know . The only other big country of which this is not so, that the big important city is the capital, is Turkey but never were two countries more different than Turkey and America, the United States of America.

So what is the reason of it that the capital of the United States is not in its big city. The reason for it in Turkey I do not know and yet it may have something to do with the reason for it in the United States of America.

When two things are alike there is very often the same reason for it.

And now another thing not only is the capital of the country of the United States nor as in other important countries in its big city but the capital of each state is with few exceptions not in its big city of the State and that too is very strange if you stop to think about it and there must be a reason for it, it is very strange and peculiar and striking that this is so and undoubtedly it has a lot to do with how any American is an American and what his government has to do with him.

Practically no state has its capital in its biggest city, practically no biggest city of any state is its capital. There may be one or two exceptions but pretty generally this which I have said is true.

Now what does it mean why is America different in this respect from any other important country. Now the United States is an important country and its capital is not in its or in any of its big cities.

And I am sure there is a very real reason for it and it has a lot to do with what Americans are and what the government is and how

73

it has worked and even perhaps it has something to do with how it does work.

Now if anybody begins to think about it what does anybody say. They may say this. I may say this.

It may be because of suspiciousness because the country was going to be suspicious of what its capital was going to do.

It may that its country does not need its capital does not need any of its capitals and likes them to be tucked away so that they won't know where they are.

It may be because things change in America or they feel they might and they like to feel that the big city may be here today and there tomorrow and if you put the capital into any big city perhaps the big city may have moved away.

That is some of the way anybody can feel about it, about the very strange fact that the capital is not where any other important country would put it.

To me the having put the capital away, just left it where nobody would notice it unless they happened to be looking for it is a very important part of what makes the country that is the people of this country what they are.

First the suspiciousness. Yes Americans are suspicious. What is the matter with it is a natural thing to say, show me I'm from Missouri is a natural thing to say. Americans are very friendly and very suspicious, that is what Americans are and that is what always upsets the foreigner, who deals with them, they are so friendly how can they be so suspicious and they are so suspicious how can they be so friendly but they just are and that certainly has something to do with their having tucked their capital, their capitals away.

But there is something more important very much more important about it than being just suspicious. There is the fact that they do not feel the need of a government and so why put it where they can always know where it is.

This is what I think they really have felt about it and that is why perhaps until now they have not needed it. Lincoln in his time said this country is sick and he was the doctor that was to make it well. That is the way America has always felt about government, a healthy man does not have to know where the doctor lives, he does know but he does not have to know and that is why they have put the capitals where they are so that they need not have them unless they need them. In wandering about the country these days I had more that same impression, the country had had a feeling that it was most awfully sick it had so many symptoms it had so

74

much the matter with it it did have to have a doctor and so they all tremendously remembered where the capital is. Now perhaps they wonder did they have to have the doctor and were they so sick and they wonder do they want to take the medicine that they so badly wanted the doctor to give them.

That is the way the American is and that is the reason I think that they tuck their capitals away.

There is another thing about Americans. And it has to do with the way they want their capital, do Americans have they ever felt that they were employed when they were hired. They used not to feel so. All Americans perhaps they have changed now but I hope not all Americans have always felt that they were not employed but that they were hired which is an entirely different thing. Have they been slowly changing, I have been afraid these last years that is before the depression that they were changing, that they were getting to be not like a hired man but like an employee, that is some one whom some one employs. There is a difference and this difference has always been American and now that the depression has come in a funny way they seem to be going back again, back to being a hired man and not an employed one, at least I hope so.

And this also has something to do with their having wanted the capital to be tucked away where they would not know that it was going on.

There is nothing that makes any one know more quickly that they are employees that is that they are employed and not on their own or a hired man than when the government is where everybody always knows about it.

I think all this is so and perhaps now the depression will make them commence again to begin again forgetting that the government is something that any one of them can know is there all the time.

It is a funny thing to feel that way about the depression but I do.

So these are some of the reasons why the American different from any other important country always has put his capital away so that when they are in their big city it will not always be there in their way, that it will not always be there to stay.

And this then is the last perhaps reason why the American has not wanted his capital in a big city because after all in any case a big city is a big city because it is a big city, but often big cities become other kinds of cities and other kinds of cities which are not big cities come to be big cities. But capitals will not become big cities important cities of that the American is sure, and he has so carefully selected where to put them the capitals so he can be absolutely sure.

And this is what an American is one who moves around and if he moves around, he knows that big cities can move around but that capitals can't. That is one thing capitals mostly always do not do they do not move.

Perhaps this is where the resemblance with Turkey comes in, that the Turks also think about moving around and so they do not want their capital to be in their way, perhaps so.

At any rate when in an airplane America is there underneath, the symmetry America has there underneath is one that although there are no more Indians red Indians living here, the symmetry of living the way they did is still here. And the Indians moved around, so does the American symmetry when it is there underneath and it is clear. It is a country made in which to move around.

It is big and so it is a good country in which to move around, and every time you go up a hill you are up and there is a little flat and then it goes down and there is so much water that if it is necessary to change from water to land and land to water there is no trouble. Nobody could ever believe there could be so much water anywhere on land as there is everywhere where there is the United States of America. This makes it a very necessary thing to know the difference between anywhere and anywhere and it makes it very easy and very solid to go anywhere and that is what Americans do do, and so why do they want their capital in a big city. They do not and they never do they never do want to have a big city as a capital. If it were not so much the habit of a country to have a capital perhaps they would not have a capital at all.

After all each one of the capitals they have is so very small, might they not just as easily not have a capital at all.

That is what it comes to if they move around a great deal and are suspicious and friendly and friendly and suspicious and if they do not ever want to be an employee but be themselves or a hired man. They want to be by themselves or be a hired man, they do not want to be an employee and so perhaps they do not need a capital at all.

Do they, do they need a capital at all.

At any rate they need a capital to be very small.

They need a capital to be very small if they need to have a capital at all.

That is what I think the depression has begun. And it would be nice if it having begun not any one would ever know what they had done with any of the capitals which the country one by one had made to be a very little one.

1935

AMERICAN STATES AND CITIES AND HOW THEY DIFFER FROM EACH OTHER

It was a natural thing that I once and that was long ago wrote about how Iowa differed from Kansas and Kansas from Ohio and Ohio from Illinois and Illinois from Michigan and that I called that writing Useful Knowledge. Not that that was useful to me not useful to use but it was just useful knowledge. I wrote it then because I always do I always did I always have asked every American every casual American I ever met, I always asked him what state did he come from and I used to think I still do think that I really ought to have known without asking him and that asking him ought only to have been confirming what I know what I knew. That is what Useful Knowledge might be confirming what you know and this might have been true.

That is all always done now and it also was always done then and quite long ago.

And then the Great War came and the American army was there that is in France and I was there and I met a great many more Americans that I ever thought any one could meet even if they were in America, and I asked them all I asked every one of them what state they were from and how they had come to go from one state to another one and of course how old they were in one and in the other one and how old they were now. I never can help wanting to know all that.

And now I am in America again, and I am once more and more than ever certain that any state and any city in that state is different in everything that is anything from any other state or any other city even if they are bordering the states or the cities take New York and Brooklyn and that is very strange and as I flew over them over the states over a good many of them very shortly after I had come back again I felt all this thing.

As I flew over them I felt that I did know really know when we passed from one state to another one of them I really was certain that I did know this thing and I wanted to write an opera about the states differing as I flew over them. It would make a very interesting opera states instead of saints. Well anyway now I have been in a great many of them and I am going to be very soon in some more of them.

There is nothing that I have ever seen or heard in Europe that has been to me so romantic as when in Oakland California when I was young we went to the railroad station just to get an ordinary local and the man said in a loud voice not to us but to a great many others this way for all points East. It is still for me a romance to be starting for all points East or West or South or North and each one of them a different city and a different state and all of them American.

And so really I have seen a good many of them states and cities and this is what I feel about them and I will even tell the name of a good many of them.

Now what is American, in which all America has something. Well it is in the fact that the cheapest thing they make is always made of the best materials. Now in all older civilizations it always has ben the other way around, the more expensive the thing the better raw material goes into it, the more expensive a thing the finer designing goes into it, but the American thing is that the cheaper a thing is to be the better the raw material has to be to make that thing like a Ford car, in the beginning or anything in America that is the cheapest and sold the most and the same is true in designing, the ten cent stores can get the best designers because they make the largest quantity of anything.

It is very interesting.

When the American army came to France they brought with them the things we had seen advertised in American magazines for many years but had never seen soaps and cigarettes, it was quite an excitement to us to really see actually really see a package of Lucky Strikes or Camel cigarettes, it was not quite romantic but it was exciting it made real something we had only seen as pictures but when I came over here and met at the Dutch treat club all the men critics and columnists and Saturday Evening Post writers and comic cartoon makers it was getting near to romance, their names were so familiar to me and it was rather unreal really seeing them actually there where they naturally were. And there is the eating of Carolina rice in North Carolina. But it was not yet really romantic and so I found out gradually that things and people are not enough to make romance and then I did find things that were to me really romantic like Europe had been romantic and now I will tell all about it.

And so how many states have I really seen this time. To begin with New York, you might call that a city and not a state but all the same I call it a state, then there is Boson and Massachusetts and

Springfield and Deerfield in Massachusetts, in short there is the whole of Massachusetts, and that was romantic to me once when I went to college at Radcliffe when I first came East from California but not now no not now. Then there is Pennsylvania and flying over that is very interesting but not quite romantic and later I will mention the reason why, there are several reasons and one of them is that I was born there. Then there is Maryland and Washington, D.C. and Chicago and Illinois and Ohio and a great many places in Ohio and Wisconsin and Minnesota and Indiana and Michigan, I have flown over a great many others but these are the principal ones over which I have been, and now there is going to be Virginia and North and South Carolina and Alabama and Louisiana that is New Orleans and then perhaps Missouri and Arizona and Texas and California, perhaps not any more than all that perhaps not.

And they are all each one of them very different from any other one of them, anybody would expect Texas to be different from Michigan but would they expect Indiana to be so different from Ohio and Ohio from Illinois and Illinois from Iowa.

And now what is the difference between Cleveland and Toledo and Columbus, Ohio, one from the other one and all of them from Indiana, Connecticut, and Massachusetts and Rhode Island are each one different from the other one. It is a strange thing that arbitrary divisions make one different from the other one only the divisions are not arbitrary as each one of them have come to be different. It makes you feel a lot to feel that.

And I have been feeling that a lot.

Seeing the actual territory of them of each state that is different makes you feel differently about them it is the same as meeting any one who comes from them. The people make you feel what the state is what the city is in one way and seeing the actual physical ground and country and building of the cities and the color and the lay of the land and the things growing on it and the way the city is built and the amount of water lakes rivers marshes and ponds or sea connected with it makes you feel each state as completely inside in it, it really has nothing to do with the state next to it although all of them are alike in having what they all have connected with it that is with them the habits and character of being American.

One state is ruled off from another state on the map the map of the United States as any one might rule it off with any common ruler rule it off straight. That is what makes the map of the United States such a fascinating map to look at the way they the states have their state line run so straight and the angles are so straight, it is only when they hit the ocean that they are not so straight.

Now that all this is said I am going from state to state with the life they led and I led within that state and wihin the cities of that state.

But first to see why this can be as romantic in its way as Europe is in its way and that is because back of the people and the things they have is the physical aspect of the land they use.

After all anybody is as their land and air is. Anybody is as the sky is low or high, and the air heavy or clear, anybody is as there is wind or no wind there. It is that which makes them and the arts they make and the work they do and the way they eat and the way they drink and the way they learn and everything.

The things that used to be the romantic thing indians and cow boys and those things to any American are not really now romantic things. And to any American in coming back to America other things are not romantic any more, gangsters or speak easies, the thing that has come to be the romantic thing for an American coming back to America and wandering are the ordinary ways of living the ways that the states and the cities have come to have as their natural thing, it is that that is the romantic thing to an American coming back to America. The fact that they all talk American, that strikes one as it does the American going to France that they all talk French. Then the simple things they do which have come to be in the every day living and writing of the country when the returned American sees that the every day things they do it is that that makes him feel romantic and then there is the particular thing. When you see the home town of a manufactured thing and the place they make it being so simply where it belongs like the Champion spark plugs in Toledo the McCormick farm implements in Chicago not to mention the Ford car being at home in Detroit Michigan all that makes you feel it is strange and real and there and therefore romantic and when you pass Marion Ohio unexpectedly and you know the book Mr. Harding or Wilbur Wright's picture field or are taken out to Edison's studio it is that that makes you feel that it is natural and strange and there and therefore romantic and not at all as you had expected although exactly as you have been told.

As we came up the bay and landed in New York they all said and the sky line but I did not look at that because it was as I remembered it and had seen it it did not feel different and so it was not romantic but when I saw the Rockefeller Center tower well that was what I had been told it was and as the pictures of it were but

it did feel different there where it was and therefore it was romantic and when one saw it suddenly from the sidewalk it made one
feel funny feel unreal and so it was romantic. And so were the
streets of New York of course they were.

And then we went west and then I began to begin to know what I
now do know about the physical aspects of the land, the water is a
part of the land, it is not land and water it is water in the land, that
is what makes it American. And that is what makes it so real and
so strange and so detailed and so there and so romantic.

I soon found the people looking different in different states. In
some the heads are rounder in some states the heads are longer, in
some the eyes were more sunken in the head near the nose in some
the features were put on outside the head, and each state was getting to be different one from the other. Anybody look at everybody
on the streets in their state and they will see that in general heads
are more or less a shape features are more or less a shape and the
way the eyes are placed in the head deep or not is more or less the
same throughout the state. Anybody can look at everybody in their
state and can then see whether they can see it as it is. Now all this
has to do with what the land looks like and what it can grow.

Indianapolis I so well remember and Toledo and Detroit, then
there is Madison Wisconsin Minneapolis and Minnesota. Then there
was the thing that was perhaps the most disappointing and that was
that when we saw the Mississippi first it was so small. Of course it
was alright that it should be because it was very near to where it was
not to be at all that is where it begins but all the same the first time
that we saw the Mississippi River it was small.

And going through Virginia there are no habitations. That makes
Virginia that Virginians have not made Virginia but it has been
left alone by them to be what it was. That is not at all true of Deerfield of Connecticut or of Massachusetts anybody can know about
that. And then there is the difference between Virginia or North
Carolina and they are so completely different Virginia or North
Carolina in houses and people and everything.

I have often thought about whether people like things difficult or
easy.

Now Indianapolis does not like things easy. Well I think a great
many states do not like things easy. I think that it has been thought
that anybody does like things to be easy but do they. Easy things
make confusion even if you let them alone.

I was reading a calendar of the political speeches made lately
and I was extraordinarily struck with it it was so difficult to know

what they meant by what they said because the words they use are so long and they embrace so many different kinds of feelings, but long words feel like something and after all that something is what long words are and is that an easy or a hard something.

And going over and on all that country the presidential timber country I wondered do they want that it should be that everything should be easy or that it should not. And I still wonder about that.

1935

AMERICAN FOOD AND
AMERICAN HOUSES

Food always remains the same after all it has to be made of flour and butter and eggs and water and meat and fowls and game and fish and shell fish and vegetables and fruit and you have to eat it raw or you have to eat it cooked and that is all there is about it and everybody changes a lot about what they do eat, it gets to be a cause, of course there is also salt and pepper and mustard and herbs, and then there are new kinds of fruit, not new kinds of meat and fowls and eggs and butter that is a more difficult matter but new kinds of vegetables and fruit, and then there are oils and vinegar and lemons and sugar, there are quite a lot of new kinds of sugar and then there is honey and maple sugar and then besides it all being raw or being cooked there is it all being hot or being cold or even perhaps being tepid, and there is milk and cream and coffee and chocolate. Well there are really quite a number of things to eat and everybody likes it all very much and then they do not like it at all and then they change their minds about it all and then they begin an entirely different way and still always in spite of all the changes the American way is a different way from the French way it really is and that is what I have to say.

As I say the American way is different from the French way and the French way is different from the Italian or the Spanish or the German or the English way. The United States way I imagine is different from the Canadian way I have never been in Canada the Canadian way of eating, and one state is different from another state's way to a certain degree but in general the American way of eating as to what they eat and the order in which they eat it and what they drink with it is the American way.

No long ago a reporter asked me what are your French friends going to ask you about America. I said do you really want to know what they are going to ask me and are going to keep on asking me about America it is about what we ate over there.

It is different very different even from what we expected the food we eat we have gotten to like it it is going to be a shock to our French friends to hear that we do like it and that it does agree with us because it is not at all food as they understand it as they always understood food.

Some of our older French friends who had at one time or another been in America when we said but what did you eat over
there, they just threw their hands up into the air and got excited.

Then when we got them calmed down all that they could say was
that it was frightful but they could remember nothing, they said
you could not remember you could remember nothing because
nothing came in any kind of order, and that was the most awful it
might all come at once, everything might all come at once on the
table and on your plate and there seemed no real distinction between a thing being cooked and raw not in America and any way
it was awful and they were all thin when they came home from
America and excited and really anybody could know that this was
so. They really were.

The country in the French country where we live in the summer
is a part of France where they are quite certain that they eat better
that the food is better that they know more about food being cooked
than in any other part of France and besides it is or was the home
of Brillat Savarin who wrote the greatest book about French eating
and so certainly it is the place where the food is the best food to be
eaten in France. Of this they are all quite certain. Madame Raca-
mier too came from that part of France where we always spend our
summers and so did the poet Lamartine and they both liked to eat
well so it would seem and so that again makes it mean that you eat
better there than anywhere else in France and of course to any
Frenchman that does mean that you eat better there than anywhere.

Madame Recamier had no children but she had had a niece and
her niece married a man named Monsieur Lenormant and he had
a son and that son's grandson is now just eighteen and his father is
a well known surgeon. The boy eighteen the son is very observing
and a patient of his father asked him to go to America with him
for two weeks and Henri was of course delighted and went. When
he came back we all asked him everything and he was there for
only two weeks but we all asked him what he ate and was it as
frightful as the older French people said and what he had to say
about it.

Well he said you see why Frenchmen do not like it the food in
America is because the food is moist. What do you mean we all
said. Well he said it is just that, the food is moist, it is very good
material much better material than they use in France, the eggs are
better the butter very good and the milk much better than in France,
the meat much much better than in France the fowls perhaps not
as good as grow in France and it is all well and honestly cooked

and all served together of course not separately as in France each kind of thing separately and the fruit is better than in France, the vegetables not so good but when you eat it it is all moist.

You see he said French people did not like food moist, if it is moist then how can they drink wine, if the food is not dry there is no reason for drinking wine. Now he said when anything is roasted in America it is juicy and if it is juicy it is moist and if it is moist you do not want to drink wine with it. Their salads made of fruit are juicy and moist and again you do not want to drink wine with it. Their dessert is mostly ice cream and that too is moist and so nobody wants to drink wine with it and to a Frenchman if you cannot drink wine you cannot dine.

We were much struck by what he said and then we came to America and he was right and there is no doubt about it compared with France the food is moist and as it is moist it is not necessary to drink wine with it indeed wine really does not go with it.

There are two things that are very striking when you come back. In the first place desserts have disappeared out of America and the lots of cakes. Salads fruit salads have immensely taken their place. We used always to tell our French friends how many different kinds of desserts how many different kinds of cakes there were in America and how there was no end to the changes in them well that is not true any more not in the North not in the South not in the East not in the Middle West, no that is not true of American eating now anywhere, all kinds of fruit salads have taken their place the place of cake and pudding which make desserts. Then there used to be so many kinds of pancakes, every kind of pancake, that too has disappeared the pancake has pretty well disappeared and I imagine that there are lots of little Americans who have never even heard of them never even heard of the word pancakes. Then in the old days there were very few soups and not really good ones. Now there are lots of kinds of soups and all very good ones.

Then there were the heavy American breakfasts, they have entirely disappeared, nobody seems to need or eat them just what has taken their place well that seems hard to say but they have disappeared and nobody seems to be offered them or want them. Perhaps in the country they still have them but most likely not but certainly not anywhere in a city.

Nevertheless the young Frenchman was right, whatever the changes are and there are certainly very many of them whatever the changes are, the one thing remains characteristic of it that the eating is moist.

I remember in 1920 a Frenchwoman weeping because she could find no lettuce anywhere in the Middle West in America not a single one and now you can go nowhere without their insisting upon you having them.

They always drank a good deal of coffee but they do now drink a perfectly extraordinary quantity of coffee. They used to drink cocoa then but that like desserts and pancakes seems to have been entirely forgotten.

So then that is that for the food and it is very interesting. The order in which it is eaten well that seems to be a matter that is to suit the individual eater and that is a terrifying thing to any Frenchman, the order in France is fixed as fixed as anything is existing.

One finds oneself doing strange things. In the old days a girl might have found herself ordering a succession of sweets, now they might begin with tomato juice and follow by a salad and then a water ice, or a man begins with cranberry juice and ham and eggs and then a fruit salad, the only thing that has really and truly remained is pie. They do have pie, they all do have pie, they do not all eat pie, there are a very great many who never eat pie, but anywhere and everywhere if you want pie you can have pie. That is really the only thing really left over.

They eat much less solid meat, meat is still what they eat but it is not such solid meat, mutton chops are tender and small pork is good but not always, but beef is very good but as I say on the whole meat is not so heavily eaten as it was.

Now what has all this to do with anything, well anything always has something to do with something and nothing is more interesting than that something that you eat.

I suppose there are lots of things that have had to do with these changes. In the first place women got tired of doing so much cooking, then, after all even a whole nation can get tired of sweets and now that the country has settled down to really living they do not need the sweets to be so stimulating. Then also as the houses got warmer by central heating sugars were not so necessary for the systems heating.

The thing that either has changed or that I have forgotten perhaps it has changed and perhaps I have forgotten, when I come to think about it I do think that I have perhaps forgotten but at any rate is has nothing at all to do with eating are the boxes they put out for the postman on the road the rural delivery. I cannot get used to them, they are such a strange decoration as they sit there on the road side resting on nothing which is a stick to support them.

These boxes are never closed they are always open practically any of them are open and it seems to trusting. Is there no neighbor to wonder or a total stranger to wonder who is doing the letter writing to whom and then to find out about it by looking. It seems so trusting to have all these letter boxes standing there by themselves perilously supported on a stick sometimes one all alone and sometimes a group of them and all of them so that anybody might take them away and everybody could see inside and see that they were open and what is inside of any letter in any one of them. All these things are so trusting and that makes the fascination of the American character, it has so much suspicion in it of anything and everything and it is so trusting, which is really very exciting of it to be.

The thing really that has changed least to my remembering are the little wooden houses in which everybody lives and these too have changed a lot I suppose at least they seem to me to be so much more open than they used to be.

I do not suppose I will ever be able to keep away from the subject of the houses being open so that anybody in passing can see everything. Nobody does look I suppose but still after all they might.

I took a walk one evening in Springfield and I found it more and more astonishing, people were sitting in a room talking and the blinds up, or eating and the blinds up. I said to my Springfield friend but suppose somebody suddenly got angry about something as they would in France and began to quarrel and stamp around and perhaps throw things about does not that ever happen. I do not think so said my Springfield friend and if it did they would before it did happen they would pull down the curtain.

I was still bothered by this when I came to the South and there I again asked the question. I said Southerners might have a sudden emotion and as they are not a careful people they would not think of pulling down the curtain. Oh said my Southern friend nobody would think of looking even if anything were happening because if he did he would be known as Peeping Tom and that he would not care to have happen.

I like to think of all these millions of houses each one by itself each one all open each one with the moist food made of good material and each one with the American family inside it really not really afraid of anything in spite of everything in the way of woods and weather and snow and sun and hurricanes and thunder and blizzards and anything.

There are a great many things I like to look at and I wonder very often if it is not the most natural thing in the world to be an American.

1935

AMERICAN NEWSPAPERS

What do they want to know in the newspapers that is what does anybody want to know just anybody and do they want to know what they do want to know or do they only think so only think they want to know what they do want to know from the newspaper because if they do if they only think so then they do get what they want. What they want or think they want to know what they want in the newspapers is to know every day what happened the day before and so get the feeling that it has happened on that day the same day and not on the day before. That is what the American newspaper is supposed to do to make it be as if they the newspapers had it to do that is to make the things that happened yesterday happen to-day.

And do they do so.

Not if you know it not if anybody knows it that it all did happen the day before.

Think of any news that is fit to print it all did happen the day before and once it is the day before it might just as well be the week before or the month before or the year before if you really do know that it was not on the day the newspaper day that it happened but on the day before. It always has happened on the day before because the newspaper cannot come out on the day it happens, of course it cannot.

When the yellow press began, I can remember when the yellow press began that was about thirty-five years ago or so. Anybody knows what the yellow press did. The yellow press that is really the American press then had in every way by headlines by scare lines, by short lines and by long lines, by making all the noise and sound they could with their words and lines tried to invent in every way they could making it be as if the news that had happened on one day had happened not on that one day but on the day the newspaper day. And they did and they did do it they almost did do it and they almost make it come to be that what happened six hours earlier was what happened six hours later. They did just that.

And now what do they do the newspapers now do, they go on as if they still were doing just that but slowly they only act as if they were doing just that acting as if it were to-day the newspaper day that everything happend and not yesterday. They have forgotten newspapers have they have forgotten to act as if it were like that as if yesterday was to-day, they have once more fallen into the fact the real fact that the news that they put in the newspapers was yesterdays news and so it is flat the news is flat just that or they still keep on using the way that the yellow press invented to make yesterdays news be as if happened to-day in the newspapers to-day.

Some country newspapers, by country I mean twenty or thirty thousand inhabitants in a city, do make yesterdays news be to-days, because everybody knows everybody and so they the newspaper make yesterdays or last weeks news sound like to-day. That is because everybody knows everybody knows about everybody every day, and as they know all the streets in town and all the people in the town any news is such real news that even if it happened yesterday it is as if it did really happen to-day so that is what they say and so it all really happens the news in the small town newspaper happens as if it happened to-day. The other news they accept as if it happened any past day preferably yesterday but really any past day.

There was a strange thing about that in the story of the birth of the quintettes and their doctor coming to New York.

That interested the reader of the metropolitan paper as if it had been the news of a small town paper. I watched some reading this metropolitan paper and they read the paper in their way but they did not settle down to reading their newspaper as if it were a real story of a real happening and a real present happening until they came to the story of the quintettes, that and the cross word puzzle was the only solid satisfaction in the metropolitan newspaper that made like a small town newspaper a real happening of to-day as to-day is as any one can say it in saying it as any one can know in knowing it.

Now the big newspaper the big city newspaper cannot do that, they cannot do that unless something is most terribly exciting and by terribly exciting it can only be terribly exciting if somebody who would excite everybody any day is mixed up with it, and that does not happen very often. Dillinger and Lindbergh were and are exciting in that way and that is not because the story their story is exciting it is exciting their story but what is really exciting is that they are exciting and that is the reason that what happens to them yesterday is still what happens to them to-day because they are existing every day and exciting every day and every day they are existing

90

they are exciting and so any day any newspaper tells anything about them it makes it like to-day and so be exciting. But there is very little that is as exciting as that that has anybody in it who is as exciting as that so most of the news the newspaper prints is the news of yesterday and not the news of to-day and so the newspaper does not do what it says it does it does not tell the news of to-day.

And what is the difference well the difference is that it is a mistake. If the newspaper says that it is printing yesterdays news as if it were the news of to-day then they are they really are a newspaper otherwise they are not.

As I say the yellow newspaper the yellow press, the American newspaper as it was invented up to to-day did try to do it and they did they did do it but that was when they invented it when invented it over thirty-five years go, you can see that the newspapers to-day which keep up the same machinery that was invented thirty-five years ago know that they do not do it. They turn their newspapers into magazines, they make them bigger and bigger until at last anybody can know that anything as big as that could not be anything that could happen to-day. Of course one might say an awful lot can happen to-day so a newspaper might be as big as that and happen to-day but it would have to be an awfully lively newspaper to be as big as that and all happen to-day so what really happens is that the metropolitan newspaper just knows it is that, that it all did happen yesterday, at best they can say it only did happen yesterday that is it only did happen six hours ago that is really the very best that they can say about any day.

Well and what should the newspaper do, well sooner or later they will have to rediscover to-day and realise that yesterday is not to-day. The small newspapers do do it somewhat in their way because everybody knows everybody and knows the exact spot where anything that happened yesterday happen to-day but what can the metropolitan newspaper do about it, well if they are going to be as big as the metropolis where they are to be to-day they must find out how they make to-day to-day and not yesterday. And how to make yesterday to-day and not yesterday.

As long as they keep on in this way, in the way they are now they are no longer newspapers that is newspapers that to-day print the news of to-day.

When the yellow press, and to-days respectable press does use the form the headlines, the sound all this their accepted ways their completely accepted way are the ways of the past exciting yellow press, but the press that yellow press had found out a way to make

91

yesterday news be to-days and when the yellow press did this it was with the idea that a newspaper should do this should make yesterdays news be to-days.

Perhaps now that is not yes that is not what the metropolitan press thinks should be the metropolitan press perhaps now the press the metropolitan press thinks that metropolitan press should be a soothing press, that it should make of the news of to-day not the news of to-day but the rest, the rest away and to the news of any day. They use the machinery of the yellow press but they do not excite anyone with it no. They almost do do this, yes they almost do do this and then it happens that it comes across them that they use the machinery of that old yellow press which they are and that this old yellow press was made and is with the hope that any news which is to come to press must be the to-days news and not that of any other day, yesterday or any other day. Yes the metropolitan press has stirring just a little in with the soothing of its yesterdays press the memory that its machinery was invented to make yesterdays news be to-days news yes to-days. So the newspaper the metropolitan newspaper gets so large that yes it mostly is soothing because that is perhaps that is what the metropolitan reading likes I guess yes it is because the comic strips are that they are just soothing. And the yellow press now that all that filled it to be exciting has come to be machinery yes that machinery now that it works as if it was something that had never been anything else, well yes now it is soothing.

There are some hang overs, some rather sweet really sweet hang overs and they are rather touching these sweet hang overs. They are mostly reporters.

Reporters are nice they are nice they are sweet they often are young and though they are supposed to ask questions they do like to talk, and I like to question and I like to listen to any one who answers questions so I get the reporters to talk that is to tell me what they are and they are reporters and they know what reporters are but they are all nice reporters and they all tell me what they are.

Now what I mean by hang over from the yellow press day is this that reporters always think they bombard you with questions but they do not they mostly talk a little and answer questions and you talk a little a good deal and more or less do not answer questions. But as I say there was the yellow press and so there is the violence of the yellow press words but as I say the metropolitan newspaper must be soothing it must be yesterdays news, and so no matter how

92

pleasant and gentle and pleasant any reporter is he must have the emotion of the violence that was once the yellow press, they still have the machinery of it, the headlines the bombarding with questions, but actually what they want is a pleasant conversation these reporters and then to write down the same general thing that was always written down about the one reported.

You must not change the tone nor the words that succeed each other, the same words must always come one after the other because the newspaper reader must not have a shock of change. To-days news must be yesterdays news, do you see how it can gradually come to that. That is the swing of the pendulum. In the old days before the yellow press yesterdays news, and everybody knew that, yesterdays news or earlier last weeks news or earlier six weeks ago news was six weeks ago news or last weeks news or yesterdays news.

Then the yellow press made yesterdays news be to-days news, they almost make it be to-morrows news and now the metropolitan press makes todays news be yesterdays news almost makes to-days news be six weeks ago's news. That is what has happened by the yellow press having become stereotyped having become a way of doing a machinery that all the schools of journalism teach and as soon as anybody can teach it it is a way of doing a thing and is not the thing itself and it begins to move backward. And this is what is, what now is, and I have enjoyed watching it and I now am enjoying telling it, and this is what just now the newspaper the American newspaper is.

Let me explain just a litle more what I mean. Think of the whole business, what the newspaper says about anything, it always every time it mentions anybody or anything it has to say the same thing using the same words otherwise it would be a shock to the newspaper reader who has gotten used to this formula about this thing, think of Will Rogers, or the comic strips or what they say about me. If they want to change they have to change so imperceptibly that the reader will not know it. That is what makes to-days news be six weeks ago news, and that is what I mean and anybody can see that what I mean that is what I say is what is is what the newspaper to-day and by to-day I mean any day of any of these days is.

1935

AMERICAN EDUCATION AND COLLEGES

Education is thought about and as it is thought about it is being done it is being done in the way it is thought about, which is not true of almost anything. Almost anything is not done in the way it is thought about but education is it is done in the way it is thought about and that is the reason so much of it is done in New England and Switzerland. There is an extraordinary amount of it done in New England and in Switzerland.

In New England they have done it they do do it they will do it and they do it in every way in which education can be thought about.

I find education everywhere and in New England it is everywhere, it is thought about everywhere in America everywhere but only in New England is it done as much as it is thought about. And that is saying a very great deal. They do it so much in New England that they even do it more [than] it is thought about.

They say are they happy enough and have they everything that goes with it. They say are they educated enough and have they everything that goes with it. It is not so certain that they are educated enough and that they have everything that goes with it although they are educated enough and they do have everything that goes with it.

It all depends where you are and where you go and what you do whether you think all the schools are one kind of school or another kind of school. When I went to school we all thought that only those went to a private school who were not bright enough to go to an ordinary school. Others who went to school at the same time thought that everybody went to private schools and nobody went to ordinary schools. I imagine it is just as much that that is to say either way it has ever been.

Very likely education does not make very much difference.

Everybody likes or dislikes education well enough except those doing it that is those giving it and they know what education is because they give it. You always know more what a thing is if you give it than if you have it. That is why teachers are teachers in a school or anywhere.

When you go to school you go to school and when you get out of school you are out of school and from that point of view that is almost all there is to it. I myself have never thought about it never thought about kinds of education. I have talked about it but I have never thought about it but lots of people do they think about it, they talk about it of course but they think about it too. I remember when I was in college going to a place somewhere where some one was talking I think it was at a University Club and I remember that the woman addressing us said we college women we are always college girls. And I went back to college and wrote about it and said it is true and what a pity. It is one of the few things that I have ever thought about about education. I do think it rather a pity that anybody after some years have passed should be able to tell by the kind of person you are what school or college you had gone to. I do think that that is rather a pity.

I was at a very nice boys' school the other day and I know that anybody later seeing any of those boys would know that they had been at that school and I did think and I do think that that is rather a pity.

It is of course necessary that anything does something to you and a pleasant school run by very competent people can perhaps do too much to you. Anything is too much if it is anything at all. That is a way of thinking about it. But really seriously everybody and by everybody I mean anybody the time has now come when so many go to pleasant and competent schools is there not a possibility that it will make so many bodies of kinds of men and women that perhaps it may be a bother to them that they are that. May it not be necessary for them if they are to be any other thing than that kind of thing may it not be necessary that they have to begin over again later than perhaps they can begin again and perhaps may they not be not at all able even to begin again being another thing but that. Anybody can think how and what they like about this education. But after all who are the ones who are going to do educating and be educated it is just as well to think about that. After all how much does any one want any one to be different from any other one, one lot of them to be different from any other lot of them. In a great many educations in a great many countries they want one lot of them to be a very different lot from the other lot. Do we. I wonder. Do we.

Anyway educators like to do that they naturally like to do that because naturally they like to feel that they have done something and if they have done something they have done that, they have made their lot different from the other lot.

That is why people who think about education and people who educate people might as well be stopped.

Perhaps they should be stopped from doing that from making one lot of the population as different as habits and ways and education can make them from any other lot.

Thinking about education and educating has that way of thinking, and there may be a result. There sometimes has been. And who wants it. The ones educating like it, because it is that. But everybody has their feeling and a country and a government is made up by what every one in it has come to have as their way of feeling. And so do they want one lot to be made from the beginning as different from any other lot.

And now this is another thing.

For some years now college students good college students tell me they want not to go on going to college and this has surprised me because we we liked going to college and I asked them why. I said perhaps they had had freedom too soon, that is before they went to college and college was for us freedom physical and mental freedom. Now they they have been free too long and so perhaps college is not where they belong perhaps not.

If they have been free for so long, then freedom in college is not to be borne. That I did see. So I asked them perhaps it might come to mean college might come to mean that freedom was gone. Might that not be a better thing.

If college could mean to them that freedom was gone might then college not be the place where they would like to belong.

After all they have to spend some time together, after all every generation has to spend some time closely alone together and that is where they belong. And college used to mean this kind of thing to every one. But now practically all of them have spent so much time closely alone with each other before college could begin that college can not come to mean that thing.

So what else can they do. Well they have to do something else, everybody always that is every generation always has to come to do something else and I am wondering about this thing. Mostly they can choose for themselves the college to which they wish to belong. And so they commence the East goes West the West goes West or South and they may mix up the North and South and the Middle West instead of going East is beginning to go West and the North and West South. So all that may make a different thing, it may make for any of them a new freedom, if they all go in different direction to college from the direction which has been the habit of

96

those going to college to be going. That is something and they are doing this thing doing this something.

And then this brings us back to education, and who educates those who are there for their education. Well I have been to a great many colleges and I mostly like them but what do those educating think about educating does it make any difference. Does anything you learn make any difference since any way any of us all of us learn a great deal, does what we learn make any difference. There is really no one asking that since the people answering that are inevitably people teaching. So that is that.

In all the colleges where I have been talking and I have been talking at a great many colleges I find that although all the students are about the same age the effect of age in each lot of them is very different. I almost lost the sense of how old they are because each lot of them seems to be quite a different age from the other lots of them. This and the way they do and do not do what they feel as they hear is what has interested me the most.

They are very different ages in the different colleges this might be because they come from one part of the country rather than another, one might suppose that those coming from other parts of the country would seem older but this is not true, one would suppose than those coming from the cities which are larger would seem older but this is not true. One would suppose that the women would seem older than the men but this again is not always true one would suppose that the men would seem older than the women but again this is not true but what is undoubtedly true is that in some colleges you get the effect of their being older and maturer than in other ones and I wonder if there is any reason for it and I am sure there is and is it better that in their college days they should in general give the impression of being mature or not maturer. I am sure I do not know, but if so, if I do not know nevertheless it is true, they do differ they very much do they very much do differ in this in one college to another.

In one college where they did seem older, Wesleyan was its name, after the lecture was over we all talked together, and we talked about whether American men any American man did not think it was not better not to think oftener not to think at all but to do what he had to do to have success come quicker. We also talked about whether the best American the most important American was not after all one who had been a long time a failure, and we spoke of Grant and Washington and Houston, and even in a kind of a way Henry Ford and Henry James and Wilbur Wright and many another. Whether in educating and in feeling the American one might say the American since 1910 had not conceived himself as a man successfully selling, rather than a man successfully making and buying and naturally if you want to sell things your mind must be empty of everything except the thing to be sold if you want to buy and make things your mind must necessarily be full of a great many things in other words a mind that is full of many things chooses but a mind that is full of only one thing has to go on selling that thing and not choosing anything.

All this has a great deal to do with why American men feel as they do [they do] not feel that anything is anything if they are not actively engaged in selling something and it is easy to begin selling something young and so generally speaking those colleges where the young men and young women are determined to be ones more going to be going to be selling something than making or buying or giving something naturally give this impression of being young, both men and women. If you think about it you will see what I mean. I do not wish to mention anything but I do wish to say everything.

Undoubtedly then American men feel that they must be destined to sell anything and if they are to sell anything must they not be young and if they must be young must they not have the education that being young is inculcating and must they then not naturally very naturally not wish to be feeling or thinking about anything in general.

I find the different colleges very different about all this.

I am going to try teaching in order to find out really find out something about all this because I wonder a good deal about all this. I say that Americans are of two kinds the Americans who succeed young and the Americans who do not succeed young and colleges do differ very much about this thing or is it that one kind of them instinctively go to one kind of college and another kind of them go to another kind of college. Anyway this question of being young and not so young and very young does differ very much in the different colleges.

Of course many of the biggest colleges for men and the biggest colleges for women are mostly like this that they make them very young because most of them are destined to be succeeding while they are young.

And so I wonder will the American man and one might say the American women feel differently sometime sometimes about succeeding, succeeding when they are young or when they are not so

98

young if they if they do then perhaps other things will then be interesting to them and now that they go everywhere to find a college anywhere that is they go North or South and East and West and Middle West and not at all in the way they used to do is not this after all the best thing that they can do. If they do so then perhaps it does not make any difference that the people educating them think about what is to be the education of them.

After all if they see each other and meet somebody else and each generation keeps on doing that thing is not that after all everything and is not the meeting some one everything and each generation being together everything. I almost think it is and I like their new way of moving around in a new direction as being really their way this generation's way of doing that thing.

1935

AMERICAN CRIMES AND HOW THEY MATTER

I wish to think carefully and earnestly about crime about American crime and to begin I have to begin with what is not crime in order to bring in to bring him in, to bring crime in.

So to begin with what is not crime American crime.

I was thinking about a man I met in New Caanan, Connecticut. He was watched and he was watching some one who interested him and he had served in the war with the Canadians and he would not remember this because there are things to forget, even if it was not a crime to do them.

So what is crime American crime.

Ah well that is a question, and it makes every one careful to answer this question.

When you think about American crime you have to think of two things and this is one thing that in America they all learn to know any one from the outside, any one gets into the newspapers, either by being in school or by graduating or by playing a game or by going to a part or by going away or coming home, there is practically no one who does not sometime find himself and his name printed in a paper. So many people's pictures are in the paper so many people talk through the radio or sing through it or do something in it and it all makes them know themselves as any one outside knows it.

They asked us to go out one night with the homicidal squad car in Chicago and we did and although there was no crime to be found except the distant killing of Baby Face who was captured that night and all we knew about that was what the radio in the car said about it as I say we went about for three hours and there was no crime. They said rainy nights there is no homicide everybody stays at home and there is only really homicide when everybody moves around, as long as they stay home they do not unless it is a family row they do not commit homicide.

There is certainly in Chicago these days much less crime than there was perhaps also in New York perhaps not less in Virginia so they tell me, Virginia which used to be one of the slow places now that the other places have slowed down seems to be one of the lively ones in crime.

We talked together a lot about not crime but whether any one would know a criminal if one saw one in another place than where one was accustomed to see them I asked the sergeant could he tell in a town he had never been in which ones were men who could commit crimes. He said very likely he could but he also very possibly would be mistaken, then he went on, police he said almost always know why a crime has been done, they mostly always know who has done the crime at least they can they often do find out but, and then he became very silent although he went on talking, sometimes they don't and it worries them. The only thing that really worries any one, he went on, is when you don't know why any one should have killed the one who is dead why he could be killed. The other night he said a negro was killed right near where we are on a street corner he was an old man he had no money he had no family, no story, he just did odd jobs enough to keep alive he was peaceable he was just nothing and then one night quite early just on the street corner he was shot down dead, nobody saw it, nobody heard anything, nobody is interested, nobody will find out anything about it because it is of no importance to anybody.

I think a lot about American crime and about crime stories written by any one, they call them detective stories instead of crime stories and that is in a way the trouble with them they are detective stories instead of crime stories in real life they are crime stories instead of detective stories. There are very few really first-class detective stories in real life. Dillinger was one, the Hauptmann case is not one because interesting as the detective end is the crime end is the more interesting one.

Some one I once knew who was the daughter of a presbyterian clergyman said that her father who was a kindly man never ever wanted to accuse any one of anything but sometimes facts were too many for him and he would then explode and say somebody has been lying frightfully.

That is what makes the Hauptmann case so fascinating to every one, every one has a feeling that underneath everything every one has been lying frightfully and that that is something that so complicates everything that no one really can know anything by anything one does mean everything.

Every country has its own kind of crime of course it has and that is a great deal due to the kind of houses anybody lives in and the kind of things that interest most of them. The two countries France and America I know best in all these ways are very different.

When the American Doughboy the American soldier was in France the thing that worried him the thing that worried him all the time was that all the houses were all shut up with shutters that they all had walls around them and that nobody could look in. What they afraid of they used to say to us, what's the matter with them what they doing that they don't want anybody to see what they feel about it about the people next to them that they want to shut themselves up like that what they scared of anyway what can anybody do to them.

We tried to explain to them that people like to feel themselves shut in alone with their family because Europeans do not like anybody outside to come inside unless they are invited beside they like to feel that once inside they are inside and once outside they are outside and they cannot comfortably mix inside and outside.

It is true you come to America and the most extraordinary thing in all America is the little wooden houses anywhere, everywhere and no shutters and the blind up and the lights on and anybody passing can see anything that is going on.

An American who has always been an American cannot imagine how strange it is to see these American homes in what all Europe thinks of as a country crime ridden filled with lawless men and women and children and here are these thousands and millions of open houses without any protection and you can see how they strike the imagination and why the American soldiers keep asking why do they shut themselves up these Europeans what they are afraid of?

It is not only that the houses are unprotected but they leave a child alone in any room in them. There again from the European point of view that is not a possible thing, a baby any kind of a baby could not be alone in a room without somebody very close to them. That is what puzzled anybody who read in Europe about the kidnaping. Nobody understood how the baby could be in a room alone without at least somebody in a room adjoining, but when anybody said that to an American the American did not understand because they said babies children are always alone unless somebody is accidentally with them, that is a natural enough thing.

It is the way people have in their houses and the kind of houses they have that make their kind of crime and that is what makes the crime of one country so fascinating to the inhabitants of another country.

Everybody remembers a crime when nobody finds out anything about who did it and particularly where the person mixed up with it goes on living.

I know I was perfectly astonished to know that even the present generation knew the name of Lizzie Borden and that she had gone on living. There are the two kinds of crime that keep the imagination, the crime hero and the crime mystery, all the other crimes everybody forgets as soon as they find out who did them.

It is a funny thing, this thing about detective stories and the difference between them and the story of a real crime. And the trouble is just that, in the real crime it is more interesting if you do not know the answer at all as in the Halls Mill case or if there is a mystery behind the answer as in the Hauptmann case, but in the other cases however exciting the story if they find out all about who did it, and finding out who did know all about how and why he did it then nobody really can remember later about it at all about that crime and it does not go on in the common memory.

So that is one kind of crime and I always come back to the Halls-Mill crime because it had almost everything that a crime could have to make it a completely interesting one, but how could one have invented it and left it like that and not done anything how could one and if one did would it have been interesting. The Hall Mills case was one that was so completely American. Every one had so much openness and honesty and directness and nothing told anybody anything and there was no feeling that anybody was lying or anybody was refusing to tell anything but nobody really told anybody anything and that was and that is so American and so very fascinating.

The Halls Mills murder case went on and characters came and characters went and nobody really told anybody anything. It is so different with Hauptmann who is a German he is always telling somebody something, he is always hiding something but he is always telling something. We were talking about that with the Bromfields once and Mrs. Bromfield said that Mrs. Mill not telling anything showed the integrity of the American woman and the case of Lizzie Borden is the same, she held back nothing she never lied but she never told anybody anything, that is integrity and is very American. The whole case was so American, the orchard was American the surrounding family was American the person who had the pig farm and had something to say but never said anything, it was all so American, the causes which were there which were almost a poem and at the same time were filled with evil meaning, and it was all so simple so evident so subtle and so open and nobody ever really came to know anything that is a kind of a crime that means

103

something as an expression of the American character, yes if you know what I mean, yes it does if you know what I mean.

When we went around in that squad car and when there was no crime in Chicago they took us to see a walking Marathon. I had never seen any such thing and it was a strange a very strange thing to be seeing. As they went moving around in a state of sleeping they were young things and they were asleep and they kept moving, it meant anything and nothing that they fell asleep and young and touch-touching and that they were asleep and that they kept moving, and they were there to be anything that is to say they were existing as they would be to any one looking at them and of course it was not a crime that they were doing what they were doing but it might have been, it would have been they would have been the same if it was a crime for them to do as they were doing. Do you see what I mean when I say anybody in America can be a public one, and anybody in America being able to be a public one it has something to do with the hero crime and so many people are always doing this thing doing the hero crime it gets into anybody who can have his picture where it is to be seen by anybody. Of course there are so many who feel themselves to be a crime hero that practically nobody wonders that there are any, their names are like the names of Pullman cars, they make them up as easily and it is no good.

For a long time the only one any one has been able to remember is Dillinger. Dillinger got to be one so completely that his father naturally could say that he was a good boy he always had been a good son. And he was right, that makes of any American a crime hero that his father can say that he is a good boy that he has always been a good boy. If they could not say that of him he would not have been on the front page of the newspaper.

And being a killer that is a natural killer and not a mean one nor one for any other thing than just being such a one that has always been an American thing and that has nothing to do with not being a good boy or a good son.

The Al Capone crime is a different thing, that is a European thing, it is an organization to have something done but such a one cannot make crime an American thing, everybody knows what it is for and how it is done and it is not really interesting to any one, everybody knows that Dillinger was a killer but he was a killer just because he was that thing and not for any reason and that is the reason he is interesting to any one.

It does make a big difference, it is why Robin Hood lives, crime if you know the reason if you know the motive if you can understand the character if it is not a normal one is not interesting a crime in itself is not interesting it is only there and when it is there everybody has to take notice of it. It is important in that way but in every other way it is not important.

So everybody will go on feeling as they always have been feeling about crime.

1935

MONEY

Everybody now just has to make up their mind. Is money money
or isn't money money. Everybody who earns it and spends it every
day in order to live knows that money is money, anybody who votes
it to be gathered in as taxes knows money is not money. That is
what makes everybody go crazy.

Once upon a time there was a king and he was called Louis the
fifteenth. He spent money as they are spending it now. He just
spent it and spent it and one day somebody dared say something
to the king about it. Oh, he said, after me the deluge, it would last
out his time, and so what was the difference. When this king had
begun his reign he was known as Louis the Well-beloved, when he
died, nobody even stayed around to close his eyes.

But all the trouble really comes from this question is money
money. Everybody who lives on it every day knows that money is
money but the people who vote money, presidents and congress, do
not think about money that way when they vote it. I remember
when my nephew was a little boy he was out walking somewhere
and he saw a lot of horses; he came home and he said, oh papa, I
have just seen a million horses. A million, said his father, well anyway, said my nephew, I saw three. That came to be what we all used
to say when anybody used numbers that they could not count well
anyway a million or three. That is the whole point. When you earn
money and spend money every day anybody can know the difference between a million and three. But when you vote money away
there really is not any difference between a million and three. And
so everybody has to make up their mind is money money for everybody or is it not.

That is what everybody has to think about a lot or everybody is
going to be awfully unhappy, because the time does come when the
money voted comes suddenly to be money just like the money everybody earns every day and spends every day to live and when that
time comes it makes everybody very unhappy. I do wish everybody would make up their mind about money being money.

It is awfully hard for anybody to think money is money when
there is more of it than they can count. That is why there ought to
be some kind of system that money should not be voted right away.

When you spend money that you earn every day you naturally think several times before you spend more than you have, and you mostly do not. Now if there was some arrangement made that when one lot voted to spend money, that they would have to wait a long time, and another lot have to vote, before they vote again to have that money, in short, if there was any way to make a government handle money the way a father of a family has to handle money if there only was. The natural feeling of a father of a family is that when anybody asks him for money he says no. Any father of a family, any member of a family, knows all about that.

So until everybody who votes public money remembers how he feels as a father of a family, when he says no, when anybody in a family wants money, until that time comes, there is going to be a lot of trouble and some years later everybody is going to be very unhappy.

In Russia they tried to decide that money was not money, but now slowly and surely they are coming back to know that money is money.

Whether you like it or whether you do not money is money and that is all there is about it. Everybody knows it. When they earn it and spend what they earn they know it they really know that money is money and when they vote it they do not know it as money.

That is the trouble with everybody, it is awfully hard to really know what you know. When you earn it and spend it you do know the difference between three dollars and a million dollars, but when you say it and vote it, it all sounds the same. Of course it does, it would to anybody, and that is the reason they vote it and keep on voting it. So, now please, everybody, everybody everybody, please, is money money, and if it is, it ought to be the same whether it is what a father of a family earns and spends or a government, if it isn't sooner or later there is disaster.

1936

MORE ABOUT MONEY

When the parliament was invented by England long ago it was mostly done to keep the king from spending too much money.

Since then every country has a parliament but who is there to stop the parliaments from spending too much money. If anybody starts spending money they never stop themselves. If they stop, it is because somebody stops them. And who is to stop congress from spending too much money. Everybody has to think about that now.

In France the chamber has been doing the same thing spending too much money and so everybody voted for the communists hoping that the communists would stop them. Now everybody thinks that the chamber under the communists will just go on spending the money and so a great many frenchmen are thinking of getting back a king, and that the king will stop the french parliament from spending money.

That is funny. Parliament was invented to stop a king spending money and now the french are thinking of getting back a king to stop the parliament from spending all their money.

In America, where, ever since George Washington, nobody really can imagine a king, who is to stop congress from spending too much money. They will not stop themselves, that is certain. Everybody has to think about that now. Who is to stop them.

1936

STILL MORE ABOUT MONEY

One of the funny things is that when there is a great deal of unemployment you can never get any one to do any work. It was true
in England it is true in America and it is now true in France. Once
unemployment is recognized as unemployment and organized as
unemployment nobody starts to work. If you are out of work and
you find some work then you go to work. But if you are part of the
unemployed then you are part of that, and if work comes you have
to change your position from the unemployed to the employed, and
then perhaps you will have to change back again, so perhaps you
had better just stay where you are.

That is what happens.

We have given up trying to employ french people, those who
were not working were unemployed and that was no way of changing them back to work, so we took to Indo-Chinamen. Indo-Chinamen are after all frenchmen, so finally they too became part of the
unemployed. I asked one of them, his name is Trac, and why don't
any of you stay in a job when you get it. Why he said it's like this.
They get ten francs a day as unemployed. Now a Chinaman can
live on five francs a day and that gives him five francs to gamble.
The rest of the time he puts on his hat and goes out. He takes a
temporary job, which still leaves him unemployed, and buys a new
suit of clothes. Then by and by he catches cold, he goes to a hospital, free, and then he dies, and has a free coffin. All the Indo-
Chinamen in Indo-China want to come to Paris to live like that.
They call that living like frenchmen.

Everybody has to think about the unemployed getting to be that
and is there any way to stop them. Everybody has to think about
that.

1936

ALL ABOUT MONEY

It is very funny about money. The thing that differentiates man from animals is money. All animals have the same emotions and the same ways as men. Anybody who has lots of animals around knows that. But the thing no animal can do is count, and the thing no animal can know is money.

Men can count, and they do, and that is what makes them have money.

And so, as long as the earth turns around there will be men on it, and as long as there are men on it, they will count, and they will count money.

Everybody is always counting money.

The queen was in the parlor eating bread and honey the king was in his counting house counting out his money.

That is the way it is and the only trouble comes when they count money without counting it as money.

Counting is funny.

When you see a big store and see so many of each kind of anything that is in it, and on the counters, it is hard to believe that one more or less makes any difference to any one. When you see a cashier in a bank with drawers filled with money, it is hard to realize that one more or less makes any any difference. But it does, if you buy it, or if you take it away, or if you sell it, or if you make a mistake in giving it out. Of course it does. But a government, well a government does just that, it does not really believe that when there is such a lot that one more or less does make any difference. It is funny, if you buy anything well it may cost four dollars and fifty-five cents or four hundred and eighty-nine dollars or any other sum, but when government votes money it is always even money. One or five or fifteen or thirty-six more or less does not make any difference. The minute it gets to be billions it does not make any difference, fifteen or twenty-five or thirty-six more or less. Well, everybody has to think about that, because when it is made up it has to be made up by all sorts of odd numbers, everybody who pays taxes knows that, and it does make a difference.

All these odd pieces of money have to go to make that even money that is voted, but does it. It is voted even but it is collected odd. Everybody has to think about that.

1936

MY LAST ABOUT MONEY

Getting rid of the rich does end up very funnily. It is easy to get rid of the rich but it is not easy to get rid of the poor. Where-ever they have tried it they have got rid of the rich all right and so then everybody is poor and also there are there more than ever there of ever so much poorer. And that is natural enough. When there are the rich you can always take from the rich to give to the poor but when everybody is poor then you cannot take from the poor to give to the ever so much poorer and there they are.

That is the inevitable end of too much organization. That organization business is a funny story.

The beginning of the eighteenth century, after everything had been completely under feudal and religious domination, was full of a desire for individual liberty and they went at it until they thought they had it, which ended up with first the English and then the American and then the French revolution, so there they were and everybody was free and then that went on to Lincoln. Then they began inventing machinery and at the same time they found virgin lands that could be worked with machinery and so they be-gan organization, they began factory organization and laborers organization, and the more they began organization the more every-body wanted to be organized and the more they were organized the more everybody liked the slavery of being in an organization.

Just the other day I was reading a Footner detective story and the crooks who were being held together under orders under awful conditions said when somebody tried to free them sure you got to be organized these days you got to have somebody do your think-ing for you. And also the other day a very able young man, you would not have expected he would feel that way about it, wrote to me and said after all we are all glad to have Roosevelt do our thinking for us.

That is the logical end of organization and that is where the world is today, the beginning of the eighteenth century went in for freedom and ended with the beginning of the nineteenth century that went in for organization.

Now organization is getting kind of used up.

The virgin lands are getting kind of used up, the whole surface

111

of the world is known now and also the air, and everywhere you see organization killing itself by just ending in organization. The more backward countries are still excited about it because they have just heard of it but in their hearts the rest of them know the poor are always there and the very much poorer are always there and what are you going to do about it.

Organization is a failure and everywhere the world over everybody has to begin again.

What are they going to try next, what does the twenty-first century want to do about it? They certainly will not want to be organized, the twentieth century is seeing the end of that, perhaps as the virgin lands will by that time be pretty well used up, and also by that time everybody will have been as quickly everywhere as anybody can be, perhaps they will begin looking for liberty again and individually amusing themselves again and old-fashioned or dirt farming.

One thing is sure until there are rich again everybody will be poor and there will be more than ever of everybody who is even poorer.

That is sure and certain.

1936

THE WINNER LOSES, A PICTURE OF OCCUPIED FRANCE

I

We were spending the afternoon with our friends, Madame Pierlot and the d'Aiguys, in September '39 when France declared war on Germany—England had done it first. They all were upset but hopeful, but I was terribly frightened! I had been so sure there was not going to be war and here it was, it was war, and I made quite a scene. I said, "They shouldn't! They shouldn't!" and they were very sweet, and I apologized and said I was sorry but it was awful, and they comforted me—they, the French, who had so much at stake, and I had nothing at stake comparatively.

Well, that was a Sunday.

And then there was another Sunday and we were at Béon again that Sunday, and Russia came into the war and Poland was smashed, and I did not care about Poland, but it did frighten me about France—oh dear, that was another Sunday.

And then we settled down to a really wonderful winter.

We did not know that we were going to stay all winter. There is no way of heating this stone house except by open fires, and we are in the mountains, there is a great deal of snow, and it is cold; but gradually we stayed. We had some coal, enough for the kitchen stove, and one grate fire that we more or less kept burning day and night, and there is always plenty of wood here as we are in wooded mountains, so gradually we stayed the winter. The only break was a forty-eight-hour run to Paris to get our winter clothing and arrange our affairs and then we were back for the winter.

Those few hours in Paris made us realize that the country is a better place in war than a city. They grow the things to eat right where you are, so there is no privation, as taking it away is difficult, particularly in the mountains, so there was plenty of meat and potatoes and bread and honey and we had some sugar and we even had all the oranges and lemons we needed and dates; a little short in gasoline for the car, but we learned to do what we wanted with that little, so we settled down to a comfortable and pleasantly exciting winter.

I had not spent a winter in the country, in the real country, since my childhood in California and I did enjoy it; there was snow, and moonlight, and I had to saw wood. There was plenty of wood to be had, but no men to saw it; and every day Basket II, our new poodle, and I took long walks. We took them by day and we took them in the evening, and as I used to wander around the country in the dark—because of course we had the blackout and there was no light anywhere, and the soldiers at the front were indulging in a kind of red Indian warfare all that winter—I used to wonder how anybody could get near without being seen, because I did get to be able to see every bit of the road and the fields beside them, no matter how dark it was.

There were a number of people all around spending the winter unexpectedly in the country, so we had plenty of society and we talked about the war, but not too much, and we had hired a radio wireless and we listened to it, but not too much, and the winter was all too soon over.

I had plenty of detective and adventure stories to read, Aix and Chambéry had them left over, and I bought a quantity every week, and there was an English family living near Yenne and they had books too, and we supplied each other.

One of the books they had I called the Bible; it was an astrological book called *The Last Year of War*, written by one Leonardo Blake. I burnt my copy the day of the signing of the armistice, but it certainly had been an enormous comfort to us all in between.

And so gradually spring came, a nice early spring, and all the men in the village had leave for agriculture and they all came home for a month, and nobody was very uneasy and nobody talked about the war, but nobody seemed to think that anything was going to happen. We all dug in our gardens and in the fields all day and every day, and March and April wore away.

There were slight political disturbances and a little wave of uneasiness, and Paul Reynaud, as the village said, began to say that that there were not to be any more Sundays. The post-office clerks were the first to have their Sundays taken away. The village said it as a joke, "Paul Reynaud says that there are not to be any more Sundays." As country people work Sunday anyway when there is work, they said it as a joke to the children and the young boys, "Paul Reynaud says that there are not to be any Sundays any more." By that time all the men who had had an agricultural leave were gone again, and April was nearly over.

The book of astrological predictions had predicted all these things, so we were all very well satisfied.

114

Besides these astrological predictions there were others, and the ones they talked about most in the country were the predictions of the curé d'Ars. Ars is in this department of the Ain, and the curé, who died about eighty years ago, became a saint; and he had predicted that this year there would be a war and the women would have to sow the grain alone, but that the war would be over in time for the men to get in the harvest; and so when Alice Toklas sometimes worried about how hot it would be all summer with the shutters closed all the evening I said, "Do not worry, the war will be over before then; they cannot all be wrong."

So the month of March and April went on. We dug in the garden, we had a lot of soldiers in Belley, the 13th Chasseurs and the Foreign Legion being fitted out for Norway; and then Sammy Stewart sent us an American Mixmaster at Easter and that helped make the cakes which were being made then for the soldiers and everybody, and so the time went on. Then it was more troublesome, the government changed,—the book of prophecy said it would, so that was all right,—and the soldiers left for Norway; and then our servant and friend Madame Roux had her only son, who was a soldier, of course, dying of meningitis at Annecy, and we forgot everything for two weeks in her trouble and then we woke up to there being a certain uneasiness.

The book of prophecy said that the month of May was the beginning of the end of the Nazis, and it gave the dates. They were all Tuesdays—well, anyway they were mostly Tuesdays—and they were going to be bad days for the Nazis, and I read the book every night in bed and everybody telephoned to ask what the book said and what the dates were, and the month began.

The dates the book gave were absolutely the dates the things happened.

The first was the German attack on the new moon, the seventh, and that was a Tuesday.

Tuesdays had begun.

Everybody was quiet; one of the farmers' wives—the richest of the farmers and our town councilor—was the only one who said anything. She always said, "*Ils avancent toujours, ces coquins-là.*" "The rascals are always coming on," she said.

There was nothing else to say and nobody said it, and then the Germans took Sedan.

That gave us all so bad a turn that nobody said anything; they just said how do you do, and talked about the weather, and that was all—there was nothing to say.

I had been in Paris as a child of five at school, and that was only ten years after the Franco-Prussian War and the debacle which began with Sedan, and when we children swung on the chains around the Arc de Triomphe we were told that the chains were there so that no one could pass under it because the Germans had, and so the name Sedan was as terrible to me as it was to all the people around us and nobody said anything. The French are very conversational and they are always polite, but when there is really nothing to say they do not say anything. And there was nothing to say.

The next thing was that General Weygand was appointed the head of the army and he said if they could hold out a month it would be all right. Nobody said anything. Nobody mentioned Gamelin's name—nobody.

I once said to a farmer that Gamelin's nose was too short to make a good general, in France you have to have a real nose, and he laughed; there was no secrecy about anything, but there was nothing to say.

We had the habit of going to Chambéry to do our shopping once a week; we always went on Tuesdays because that suited best in every way, and so it was Tuesday, and nobody was very cheerful. We had a drink in a café. Vichy for me and pineapple joice for Alice Toklas, and we heard the radio going. "What's the news?" we asked mechanically. "Amiens has fallen," said the girl.

"Let's not believe it," I said: "you know they never hear it straight." So we went to the news bulletin, and there it was not written up, and we said to the girl in charge, "You know, they are putting out false news in the town; they told us Amiens was taken." "No," she said, "but I will go and ask." She came back; she said, "Yes, it is true."

We did not continue shopping, we just hurried home.

And then began the series of Tuesdays in which Paul Reynaud in a tragic voice told that he had something grave to announce.

That was that Tuesday.

And the next Tuesday was the treason of the Belgian king.

And he always announced it the same way, and always in the same voice.

I have never listened to the radio since.

It was so awful that it became funny.

Well, not funny, but they did all want to know if next Tuesday Paul Reynaud would have something grave to announce.

And he did.

"Oh dear, what a month of May!" I can just hear Paul Reynaud's voice saying that.

Madame Pierlot's little granddaughter said not to worry, it was the month of the Virgin, and nothing begun in the month of the Virgin could end badly; and the book of prophecy had predicted every date, but exactly. I used to read it every night; there was no mistake, but he said each one of these days was a step on in the destruction of the Third Reich, and here we were. I still believed, but here we were, one Tuesday after another; the dates were right, but oh dear!

Of course, as they were steadily advancing, the question of parachutists and bombing became more active. We had all gotten careless about lights, and wandering about, but now we were strict about lights, and we stayed at home.

II

I had begun the beginning of May to write a book for children, a book of alphabets with stories for each letter, and a book of birthdays,—each story had to have a birthday in it,—and I did get so that I could not think about the war but just about the stories I was making up for this book. I would walk in the daytime and make up stories, and I walked up and down on the terrace in the evening and made up stories, and I went to sleep making up stories, and I pretty well did succeed in keeping my mind off the war except for the three times a day when there was the French communiqué, and that always gave me a sinking feeling in my stomach, and though I slept well every morning I woke up with that funny feeling in my stomach.

The farmers who were left were formed into a guard to wander about at night with their shotguns to shoot parachutists if they came. Our local policeman, the policeman of Belley, lives in Bilignin and he had an up-to-date anti-parachutist's gun. He did not look very martial and I said to him, "What are you going to do with it?" and he said, "I—I am not afraid." Well, Frenchmen are never afraid, but they do like peace and their regular daily life. So now nobody talked about the war; there was nothing to say about that. They talked about parachutists and Italy and that was natural enough—we are right here in a corner made by Italy and Switzerland.

The women did say, "They are advancing all the time, the ras-

117

cals," but the men said nothing. They were not even sad; they just said nothing.

And so that month was almost over; and then one day, it was a Sunday, I was out walking with Basket just before lunch, and as I came up the hill Emil Rosset and the very lively servant they had, who had been with them for twenty-five years and had had a decoration and reward by the government for faithful service on a farm, and who in spite of all that is very young and lively, were standing pointing and said, "Mademoiselle! Mademoiselle! Did you see them?" "What?" I said. "The airplanes—the enemy airplanes! There they go, just behind the cloud!"

Well, I just did not see them; they had gone behind the clouds.

There were eight, they told me, and were flying very feebly.

We have a range of hills right in front of the terrace; on the other side of these hills is the Rhone, and that is where they had come from.

Of course we were all really excited; enemy airplanes in a city are depressing, but in the open country, with wooded hills all around, they are exciting.

We have several very religious families in Bilignin and one with four girls and a boy, and they all go into Belley to Mass, and Madame Tavel said to me, "I knew it,"—it was her day to stay home with the animals,—"I knew it: they always come on Sunday and burn the church." She had been a young girl in French Lorraine in the last war and met her husband there, who had been a prisoner.

"But," she said, "of course we have to go to Mass just the same."

It was she who later on said to her little girl, who was to go out into the fields with the cows and who was crying, Madame Tavel said, "Yes, my little one, you are right to cry. Weep. But, little one, the cows have to go and you with them all the same. *Tu as raison, pleures, ma petite.*"

We went over to Culoz, which is about twelve kilometres away, to see our friends and to hear the news. Culoz is the big railroad station in this part of the world where trains are made up for various directions, and there they had dropped bombs. All the veterans of Culoz turned out to see the bombs drop and they were disappointed in them; they found them to be bombs of decidedly *deuxième catégorie,* very second-rate indeed.

It was the only time we had bombs really anywhere near us, and one of the German airplanes was brought down near a friend's house not far away and a country boy seventeen years old brought

118

in the aviators, and it was a pleasant interlude, and we could all talk again and we had something to talk about and the veterans all were very pleased for the first time in this war; one of our friends remarked that it really was a *fête pour les anciens combattants*.

The war was coming nearer. The mayor of Belley came to Bilignin to tell the mothers that two of their sons were killed.

It was sad; they were each one the only sons of widows who had lost their husbands in the last war, and they were the only ones, now the war is over we know, who were killed anywhere in this countryside.

They were both hard-working quiet fellows twenty-six years old, and had gone to school together and worked together and one of them had just changed his company so as to be near the other, and now one bomb at the front had killed them both.

That month was over and June was commencing.

I had finished the child's book and had settled down to cutting the box hedges. We have what they call a *jardin de curé*, with lots of box hedges and little paths and one tall box pillar, and I found that cutting box hedges was almost as soothing as sawing wood. I walked a great deal and I cut box hedges, and every night I read the book of prophecy and went promptly to sleep.

And none of us talked about the war because there was nothing to say.

The book of prophecy once more gave the significant days for June and they were absolutely the days that the crucial events happened, only they were not the defeat of Germany but the downfall of France.

It made me feel very Shakespearean—the witches' prophecy in *Macbeth* about the woods marching and Julius Caesar and the Ides of March; the twentieth century was just like that and like nothing else.

And then Italy came into the war and then I was scared, completely scared, and my stomach felt very weak, because—well, here we were right in everybody's path; any enemy that wanted to go anywhere might easily come here. I was frightened; I woke up completely upset. And I said to Alice Toklas, "Let's go away." We went into Belley first and there there were quantities of cars passing, people getting away from Besançon, both of us and all the Belleysiens standing and looking on; and I went to the garage to have my car put in order and there were quantities of cars getting ready to leave, and we had our papers prepared to go to Bordeaux and we telephoned to the American consul in Lyon and he said,

"I'll fix up your passports. Do not hesitate—leave."

And then we began to tell Madame Roux that we could not take Basket with us and she would have to take care of him, but not to sacrifice herself to him; and she was all upset and she said she wished we were away in safety but that we would not leave, and she said the village was upset and so were we, and we went to bed intending to leave the next morning.

I read the book of predictions and went to sleep.

The next morning I said, "Well, instead of deciding let us go to see the *préfet* at Bourg and the American consul at Lyon.

We went; it was a lovely day, the drive from Bourg to Lyon was heavenly. They all said, "Leave," and I said to Alice Toklas, "Well, I don't know—it would be awfully uncomfortable and I am fussy about my food. Let's not leave." So we came back, and the village was happy and we were happy and that was all right, and I said I would not hear any more news—Alice Toklas could listen to the wireless, but as for me I was going to cut box hedges and forget the war.

Well, two days after when I woke up, Alice Toklas said sooner or later we would have to go.

I did not have much enthusiasm for leaving and we had not had our passports visaed for Spain, and the American consul had told us we could, so I said, "Let's compromise and go to Lyon again."

The car's tire was down and Madame Roux said, "You see, even the car does not want to leave."

Just then Balthus and his wife came along; they had come down from Paris, sleeping two days in their little car, and they were going to their summer home in Savoy and after, if necessary, to Switzerland, Madame Balthus being Swiss. Well, anyway we went to Lyon.

On the way back we were stopped every few minutes by the military; they were preparing to blow up bridges and were placing anti-aircraft guns and it all seemed very near and less than ever did I want to go on the road.

And at the same time when Alice Toklas would say about some place on the road, "Look, what a lovely house that is!" I said, "I do not want to look at it—it is all going to be destroyed."

So just before we got to Belley, at a little village near a little lake, there were Doctor and Madame Chaboux.

"What," said we, stopping, "are you doing here?"

"We are paying for our year's fishing rights," they said; "and you?" said they. "Well," said we, "we are trying to make up our minds what to do, go or stay."

"Now," said I, "tell me, Doctor Chaboux, what shall I do?"

"Well, we stay," said they. "Yes," said I, "but a doctor is like a soldier—he has to stay."

"Yes," said they.

"But now how about us? Should we or should we not?"

"Well," said Doctor Chaboux, reflecting, "I can't guarantee you anything, but my advice is stay. I had friends," he said, "who in the last war stayed in their homes all through the German occupation, and they saved their homes and those who left lost theirs. No," he said, "I think unless your house is actually destroyed by a bombardment, I always think the best thing to do is to stay." He went on, "Everybody knows you here; everybody likes you; we all would help you in every way. Why risk yourself among strangers?"

"Thank you," we said, "that is all we need. We stay."

So back we came and we unpacked our spare gasoline and our bags and we said to Madame Roux, "Here we are and here we stay."

And I went out for a walk and I said to one of the farmers, "We are staying."

"*Vous faites bien,*" he said, "*mademoiselle. We all said 'Why should these ladies leave? In this quiet corner they are as safe as anywhere,' and we have cows and milk and chickens and flour and we can all live and we know you will help us out in any way you can and we will do the same for you. Here in this little corner we are en famille,* and if you left, to go where?—*aller, où?"*

And they all said to me, "*Aller, où?"* and I said, "You are right—*aller, où?"*

We stayed, and dear me, I would have hated to have left.

III

The Kiddie has just written me a letter from America and he says in it, "We have been wondering what the end of war in France will mean for you, whether you could endure staying there or the exact opposite, whether you could endure not staying there."

So I said to Alice Toklas, "I am cutting the hedges, even the very tall one on a ladder, and I am not reading the prediction book any more, and I am walking and I am knowing what the news is," and Alice Toklas began making raspberry jam,—it was a wonderful raspberry hear,—and the long slow days passed away.

They did not really pass.

One day I said to her, "Ten days ago when we were in Lyon," and she said, "Nonsense, it was three days ago." Well, it seemed like ten, but the days all the same did pass one day at a time.

In the afternoons Basket and I always walked.

We walked in the country roads and every now and then a little girl would appear through the bushes; she was sitting with the cows and knitting, but when she heard us she came to the road. They are often blue-eyed, the little girls, as we are in the hills, and hills seem to make people's eyes blue, and she would say, "How do you do, Mademoiselle? *Vous êtes en promenade*—you are out for a walk," and I would say, "Yes, it is a nice day," and she would say, "Yes," and I would say, "And you are alone," and she would say, "Yes, my mother was here, but she went home—perhaps she will come again," and then she would say, "And have you heard the airplanes?" and I would say, "No, have you?" and she would say, "Oh yes," and I would say, "Were they German or French?" and she would say, "I do not know," and I would say "Perhaps they are French," and she would say, "Perhaps," and then I would say good-bye and she would say good-bye and disappear back through the bushes into the field, and it was always the same conversation and it was a comfort to us both, to each little girl and to me.

We went to Belley to buy food and the rest of the time I cut box hedges and Alice Toklas went on making raspberry jam; we had lots of raspberries; and as I did not listen to any news any more it was heavy but peaceful.

Then came the next Sunday.

I went out for a walk in the morning and stopped to talk with one of the farmers, Monsieur Tavel. "Well," said he, "the battle of Lyon has commenced." "What?" said I. "Are they at Lyon?" From then on they were always spoken of as "they"; they did not have any other name. "Yes," he said, "but it is all right; there are lots of soldiers there and it is all right." "But why is it all right?" I said. "Well," he said, "because there is an old prophecy which says that the day will come when France will be betrayed by a Catholic king, not her own king but another king—that another king will be crazy, and that all the Paris region will be occupied by the enemy and, in front of Lyon, France will be saved by a very old man on a white horse.

"Well," he said, "the king of the Belgians was a Catholic king and he betrayed us, the king of Italy has gone mad, and the Maréchal Pétain is a very old man and he always rides a white horse. So it is all right," said Monsieur Tavel.

Well, Lyon was awfully near and if there was going to be a great battle—well, anyway it was a bright sunny day, and I came back and I was tired and so I took out my deck chair and sat in the sun on the terrace and I went sound asleep. Then there was a half-past-twelve communiqué and I woke up just to hear that the Maréchal Pétain had asked for an armistice.

Well, then he had saved France and everything was over. But it wasn't, not at all—it was just beginning for us.

The village did not know what to say and nobody said anything; they just sighed; it was all very quiet.

We thought we could keep the shutters open and light the light, but they said no, not yet, the armistice was not signed and they, the Germans, might be anywhere.

The boys between sixteen and twenty—we have five of them in the village—were frightened lest they should be taken into the German army; they went to Belley to try to enlist in the French army, but naturally that could not be done. They came back with tears in their eyes and nervous. The peasants could not work—nobody did anything for a day or two. And then news commenced again; the man who bought the milk of Bilignin had met somebody who had seen the Germans and they had been quite kind—had given them gasoline for their car. They had been stuck somewhere without gasoline because, as the Germans advanced, the order had come that the gasoline should be poured away. Some did it and some did not. Belley is very law-abiding and so all the people who sold gasoline did.

The man who had the milk route which included Bilignin told them he would not come for the milk any more, nor would he pay them, but they could have three of his pigs. They had no way of getting them, so they asked me and I supplied the means of locomotion, and we brought back three pigs and somebody from Belley came out and butchered them and they gave us a beautiful big roast of pork, and with that and a ham we had bought and what there was to eat in the village we were very well fixed.

Everybody was getting more and more nervous and on Tuesday we went in to Belley; there was no armistice yet, but we thought we might get some soap and other things we needed.

We were in the biggest store in Belley, a sort of a bazaar, when all of a sudden the proprietor called out, "Go to the back of the shop!" Well, naturally we didn't and we heard a rumbling noise

123

and there two enemy machinegun tanks came rushing through the street, with the German cross painted on them.

Oh my, it did make us feel most uncommonly queer. "Let's go home," we said, and we did not do any more shopping; we went back to Bilignin.

And there we waited.

The boys between seventeen and twenty went up into the hills; they were badly frightened and excited. Their parents did not say anything. Thy had each taken with them their bicycles and a large loaf of bread. Naturally that did not last long and in two days they were back again. One of them, a boy named Roger, who was working for a farmer, was so frightened he ate nothing for three days and turned green with fright. He had two brothers in the French army—that was all right, but to be a German soldier! We all tried to cheer him up, but he sat in the corner and couldn't move.

The only news we had about Belley or about anything, because the electrity and the post office were cut off, was by way of the policeman of Belley, who lives in Bilignin. He had to go back to sleep in Belley, but he always managed to get out once during the day to see his mother and give us the news—yes, the Germans were there in Belley; yes, so far they had behaved very correctly; no, nobody knew anything about the armistice.

I remember the last newspaper the postman brought to us. I went out and said, "it is nice to see you." "I wish," said he, "that I could bring you better news, and I do not think I will come again," and he did not, not for more than three weeks.

Basket and I had begun to walk again, the cows and the children began to go out again, and then we began to hear cannon.

Every day we heard the cannon; it seemed to be all around us, which, as it turned out, it was and in some strange way we all cheered up at the sound of the cannonade.

We all began to talk about hearing the cannon, we all began to try to locate the direction of the cannon; some of the *anciens combattants* thought it came from the Alps, others thought ie came from right near by, and then one evening I smelt the brimstone, and the color of the earth in the setting sun was a very strange yellow green and there were clouds, strange clouds, the kind of clouds I had never seen before, thick yellow-green clouds rolling past the hills, and it reminded me of pictures of the Civil War, the battle of Lookout Mountain and that kind of thing—it looked like it and it smelled like it, and in a strange way it was comforting.

124

The policeman in his daily visit home told us that it was cannon and that it was all around us; the French had blown up the bridges of the Rhone all around us, some only about four kilometres away, and in all the places we knew so well there were machine guns and cannon and fighting and quantities of Germans; armored cars were going through Belley, and in all the villages around there were Germans and some motorcycle Germans came through our village.

And then came another bad Sunday; some of the children went in to Mass and came back with an exciting story that everybody that had any gasoline in their possession was going to be shot. Well, I had some extra gasoline besides what was in my car and I did not want to be shot. So, very nervous, I rushed off to the farmer, our neighbor, who is one of the municipal councilors of Belley, and asked what I should do. "Do nothing," he said; "unless they put up a notice here in Bilignin you do not need to do anything. Besides," said he, "I am going to Belley to find out all about it." And he came back and told us that what had happened was that Belley had gotten rid of all its gasoline and a German company had come along and they had had an accident and lost their gasoline tank, and they had asked at a garage for gasoline. Monsier Barlet, our very gentle garage keeper, had said that he had none, and the Germans had not believed him and said they would shoot him if he did not produce it, and the mayor, who is also a gentle soul, but efficient, said he would put up a notice and have the town crier announce what was happening, and everybody who had any gasoline would bring it, and everybody in Belley did, and very soon the Germans had more than they needed and everybody went home with their gasoline and Monsieur Barlet was not shot. But he was and is our local hero, and he was quite pale for some days after and we all thanked him for not being shot, and he always carries around in his pocketbook the order that was posted that saved him from being shot.

That was absolutely the only unpleasant incident that happened in Belley, and that was on the Sunday when the Germans were very nervous; they were held up at the Rhone, and as the Rhone makes many bends, and the Chasseurs Alpins were fighting hard there, they thought they were caught in a trap.

IV

Well, then came Tuesday and Wednesday, and the rain poured and poured and the notice of the signing of the armistice was signed by the mayor of Belley and the German Colonel in command there, and posted up in Bilignin. I will never forget that day. It was about noon, and Basket and I went out for a walk and there in the pouring rain sadly were the five young boys of Bilignin leaning on their sticks with which they lead their oxen; they were in the middle of the road and desperate.

Nobody else was around except one farmer's wife and she said to me, "Well, I suppose we will go on working even if we are no longer masters in our own home."

The next day was a little better. It had stopped raining and the terms of the armistice were broadcast; we once more had electricity and we knew our little corner was not going to be occupied territory, neither the Bugey nor Lyon, and we gave a sigh of relief. Monsieur Premilieu said to me, "Of course we are going to have bad days, many bad days, but it is better to bear them indirectly than directly." The boys cheered up and began to eat, and we went in to Belley to shop and, well, in short to begin to move about; and besides—happy moment—we could leave our lights burning at night and the windows and the shutters open.

Even now, a good month after it is finished, every night when I go out walking and see all the lights shining I know the difference, and I cannot help feeling sorry, particularly for the English, but even a little for the Germans who are there in the dark and afraid of bombardment.

Cannonading is not agreeable, but it is bearable, but bombing from above, and not very far above, is mighty unpleasant.

The soldiers and civilians are all agreed about that.

So we went in to Belley and there they were.

All the time they were here they were not spoken of as anything except they, *eux*.

It was impossible, but there they were, and we were seeing them.

Belley is a town of about five thousand inhabitants, a small town but important, as it is the capital of a rich county, has a hospital, a seminary, many schools, a county court, a *sous-préfecture*, and a garrison. There are also a good many convents, and so, although the population is not large, it has a number of very large buildings and feels like a small capital. It was also just about the centre of all the recent fighting, and so the Germans had made it the headquarters for all the troops in this part of the country.

So when we went in to Belley—we are about a mile out of Belley, on a small country road—we saw them, quantities of soldiers in gray uniforms, trucks, motorcycles, armored cars. We could not believe our eyes, but there they were.

126

It was not real, but there they were; it looked like photographs in a magazine but there they were.

I sat in the car and waited while Alice Toklas shopped and then she sat in the car and waited while I went to see Madame Chaboux and shopped. We always stayed, one of us, in the car because of the dogs and the car—even though the Germans were very polite and very correct. That is what everybody was saying. "They are correct."

It was strange sitting there watching the people [going] up and down on the main street of Belley, like all country towns; there are always a good many people going up and down the main street of a country town, and now added to it were these familiar and unfamiliar German soldiers, familiar because we had seen their photographs in illustrated papers all winter and unfamiliar because we never dreamed we would see them with our own eyes.

They did not look like conquerors; they were very quiet. They bought a great deal, all sugar things, cakes and candies, all silk stockings, women's shoes, beauty products and fancy soaps, but always everlastingly what the American soldiers in the last war called "eats"—that is, anything sweet—and anything that looked like champagne.

They went up and down, but they were gentle, slightly sad, polite; and their voices when they spoke—they did not seem to talk much—were low, not at all resonant.

Everything about them was exactly like the photographs we had seen except themselves; they were not the least big like we thought they would be. They admired Basket II and said to each other in German, "A beautiful dog." They were polite and considerate; they were, as the French said, correct. It was all very sad; they were sad, the French were sad, it was all sad, but not at all the way we thought it would be, not at all.

The French, the girls and boys and the older men and older women, who also went up and down about their own affairs, had that *retenue* that is French—they neither noticed nor ignored the Germans. In all the three weeks that the Germans were in Belley there was no incident of any kind.

When the Germans left, in Belley, in Yenne, in Lyon, and I imagine everywhere else in France, they thanked the mayors and congratulated them upon the extraordinary discipline of their populations. The Germans called it discipline, but it was not—it was the state of being civilized that the French call *retenue*. It was all not at all what we had feared and expected, and it all was very wonderful and very sad.

The days went on; everybody began to work in the fields, nobody had anything to say, and everybody was waiting, waiting for the Germans to go away—"they."

Everybody, when I went out walking and they were with the cows, would ask a little anxiously, "Is it eight o'clock yet?" Everybody was supposed to be at home and with the shutters closed by eight o'clock. We went into Belley quite often and it was always just that, neither more nor less than just that.

And then finally one day we went in and as we turned into the main road they whistled. We did not suppose it had anything to do with us and in a way it did not, except that nobody was supposed to be on the main roads for two days because they were leaving, and the roads were to be kept open for them. We had not stopped when they whistled, but they did not bother us; they did not, one might say, bother anyone.

And then miles and miles of them went away and they were gone.

Everybody breathed again.

Everybody began to talk again, not about anything in particular, but they all just began to talk again.

The post office was open again and everybody began to worry about everybody's husband and brother and father and nephew and son, everybody, and nobody had heard anything for so long.

Slowly they began to hear; some did not hear for a long time, but more or less they all began to hear and they all began to write all the soldiers about coming home, and they said they were coming home and they did come home.

Gradually everybody began to realize that very few Frenchmen were dead; a great many were prisoners, but very few were dead; and a great load was lifted off France. It was not like the last war, when all the men were dead or badly wounded; practically nobody was wounded and very few were dead. Everybody forgot about being defeated, it was such a relief that their men were not dead.

The Germans had said that when they were here; they said lots and lots of Germans had been killed and very, very few French.

Later on I asked the returned French soldiers how they had succeeded in killing so many Germans and not any of them being killed themselves. They explained that there was terrific aerial bombardment, but that all the soldiers had to do was lie down and the bombs exploded before they were hit. They said that the bombs were made to explode on buildings, not in the ground, and so civilians in a city like Auxerre were killed, but as the soldiers were in the open country they were not killed. Then, while the air bombardment was going on, the tanks broke through the French line, and opened out in a fan behind the French line; the German infantry, being in serried formation behind the tanks, were shot down and so a lot of them were killed, but as there were so many of them they finally exhausted the capacity of the French to kill them and they came through too, and so the French were made prisoners except a great many who made off into the fields and, walking twenty-five kilometres a day or finding a stray bicycle, got home.

Georges Rosset made it all very clear, his only regret was that he had lost all his accoutrement and particularly a very nice pair of socks that Alice Toklas had knitted for him out of very lovely wool. He wrote all about that before he managed to get home, but Alice Toklas said to his mother to write that she would immediately start another pair and anyway he would have a chocolate cake when he came home, and she did make a chocolate cake for him when he did come home, and he is home. They all are. The curé d'Ars had said that the women would plant the grain and the men would harvest it and here they were—they are harvesting it, and it is all harvested.

He also said that when everything was at its worst, then it would turn out to be at its best.

V

It is very true that all the old predictions are that there will be a complete disaster; one said that the cock would completely lose its feathers and that afterwards its feathers would be more beautiful than ever. The French do naturally not like that life is too easy, they like, like the phoenix, to rise from the ashes. They really do believe that those that win lose.

In the meantime the government of France had changed, but that did not worry anyone.

It was natural that, since the Third Republic had not defended them from their enemies, it would end.

As I said in *Paris France,* to the French a government is something outside which does not concern them; its business is policing, defending them from their enemies; it is to be hoped that it will not cost too much, and naturally it leaves everyone to lead their own French life.

And so naturally the government had changed, but their life was to go on all the same.

Everybody was happy, because their men were alive and a good many of them had come home. There were a great many difficulties, mostly concerning themselves with the question of gasoline and the question of butter.

These were the two things that bothered everybody the most.

French farmers need bread, wine, vegetables, and butter. Meat is a luxury, not a necessity, to be eaten when had, but never thought about in between; sugar and coffee a half luxury—you can do without but you miss it; but bread and wine and vegetables and butter you must have.

There was no lack of bread, wine, and vegetables; there was a moment of hesitation about bread, but the harvest was excellent, and there was no real lack; vegetables and wine are always there, and suddenly there was a question of butter. Whether it was because the Germans made such a fuss about butter that made the French think that butter could be a luxury or what I do not know, but suddenly butter became, as everybody said, *une chose rare.*

It was a puzzle—there were the same number of cows and so there was as much milk, but where was the butter?

Of course there was the trouble about gasoline. There being no gasoline, the milkmen could not make their rounds, but even so, what with bicycles and horses, milk was gathered in. But the butter?

There was a wild flurry about butter. The most sober of the farmers' wives were fussed. Their milk was under contract to go to the dairies, and the dairy would not give them butter. Nobody in France talked about anything but butter. Well, one way or another, one did get enough butter to cook with and to eat, but everybody went somewhere else to get it and it was purchased silently; it was a whole history of intrigue and it did a great deal to make everybody forget about war and about government, and then all of a sudden everybody had butter and that was over.

Everybody breathed again; everybody could have bread, butter, wine, and vegetables, and so they forgot their troubles.

They settled down to get in their harvest. Just tonight one of the wagons, with its oxen, was coming in very late at night, about ten o'clock, loaded with wheat, and I said, "It is late. Is the harvest all in?" "Yes," they said, "yes. There is our bread." It did not look like bread yet; it looked more like straw—but it was bread.

The only trouble left was the question of gasoline and that is still a trouble, and very complicated.

Of course there is none in France and they are trying to substitute for it charcoal, and that does very well for trucks, but it does not do for small cars, and how will there be any gasoline if the English keep blowing it up and besides not letting it pass?

The only way at present is not to use any, and to gather in what there is. Well, that seems to work all right, only it stopped all business, and so from time to time a day was given in which everybody who had any gasoline could go out. You could not buy any, but you could go out. And just now, the eighth of August, everybody says that everybody who has any gasoline can go about. "But," said I to Madeleine Rops, "it did not say so in the paper." "Ah, my dear," said Madeleine, "after all you do not yet understand French logic. Nobody was allowed to *rouler,* and then all of a sudden they announced that after the twenty-fifth of August nobody is allowed to *rouler.* So, *ma chère,* that means that now everybody can *rouler,* otherwise why should they say that after the twenty-fifth it will all be *contrôlé? C'est simple,*" said Madeleine Rops. So we got out the car and went shopping into Belley, most exciting; it used to be a bit of a bore to have to go shopping into Belley, but now, as it can only be done unexpectedly, it is most exciting.

And so everybody is very busy accommodating themselves to everything, and I must say the French are really happy in combining and contriving and intriguing and succeeding, and above all in saving. This evening, in going out walking, I met the town's people bringing in as much wood as they could carry; of course there are lots of woods around there and fallen branches and everybody is carrying in some for autumn burning.

I have been talking to the young people and asking them how they like it all and they said they are very pleased. They say now they can begin to feel that they have their future to create, that they were tired of the weak vices that they were all indulging in, that if they had had an easy victory the vices would have been weaker and more of them, and now—well, now there is really something to do—they have to make France itself again and there is a future; and then there is to be lots of electricity and they want France to be self-sufficing, and they think it will be and they all think that French people were getting soft, and French people should not be

131

soft. Well, anyway they are looking forward, and then besides
they won't all just go into the bureaucracy the way they were doing; they will have to find other things to do. In short, they feel
alive and like it.

The older people, once they have gotten over the shock, do not
seem to mind either; nobody seems to mind, as Madeleine Rops
said after having come all the way from Bordeaux to Belley. Really, you know, you would not think that it was a defeated country—
not at all; they seem much more wide-awake than they were.

Well, yes, they do a little regret the predictions, but still all the
predictions said that the cock would lose its feathers but would
come out more crowing than ever, and they all said that when the
worst was there the best would follow; and then there was Sainte
Odile, who said that after her blood flowed in June, four months
after, France would be more glorious than ever. Well, why not?

I had my own private prediction, and that was that when I had
cut all the box hedges in the garden the war would be all over.
Well, the box hedge is all cut now today, the eighth of August, but
the war is not all over yet. But anyway our light is lit and the
shutters are open, and perhaps everybody will find out, as the
French know so well, that the winner loses, and everybody will be,
too, like the French, that is, tremendously occupied with the business of daily living, and that that will be enough.

1940

BROADCAST AT VOIRON (EXCERPT)

What a day is today that is what a day it was day before yesterday, what a day! I can tell everybody that none of you know what this native land business is until you have been cut off from that same native land completely for years. This native land business gets you all right. Day before yesterday was a wonderful day. First we saw three Americans in a military car and we said are you Americans and they said yes and we choked and we talked, and they took us driving in their car, those long-awaited Americans, how long we have waited for them and there they were Lieutenant Olsen and Privates Landry and Hartze and then we saw another car of them and these two came home with us, I had said can't you come home with us we have to have some Americans in our house and they said they guessed the war could get along without them for a few hours and they were Colonel Perry and Private Schmalz and we talked and patted each other in that pleasant American way and everybody in the village cried out the Americans have come the Americans have come and indeed the Americans have come, they are here God bless them. Of course I asked each one of them what place they came from and the words New Hampshire and Chicago and Detroit and Denver and Delta Colorado were music in our ears. And then four newspaper men turned up, naturally you don't count newspaper men but how they and we talked we and they and they asked me to come to Voiron with them to broadcast and here I am.

. . . You know I thought I really knew France through and through but I did not realize what it could do what it did in these glorious days. Yes I knew France in the last war in the days of their victories but in this war in the days of defeat they were much greater. I can never be thankful enough that I stayed with them all these dark days, when we had to walk miles to get a little extra butter a little extra flour, when everybody somehow managed to feed themselves, when the *Maquis* under the eyes of the Germans received transported and hid the arms dropped to them by parachutes, we always wanted some of the parachute cloth as a souvenir, one girl in the village made herself a blouse of it.

It was a wonderful time it was long and it was heartbreaking

133

but every day made it longer and shorter and now thanks to the land of my birth and the land of my adoption we are free, long live France, long live America, long live the United Nations and above all long live liberty. I can tell you that liberty is the most important thing in the world more important than food and clothes more important than anything on this mortal earth, I who spent four years with the French under the German yoke tell you so.

I am so happy to be talking to America today so happy.

1944

OFF WE ALL WENT TO SEE GERMANY

I think you'd better come and make a trip over Germany said Bob Sweet. Bob Sweet is a corporal in the 441st Troop Carrier Group and he is full of ideas and I usually do whatever he tells me to do. But Bob, I said, I don't like Germans, I saw enough of them in France I don't want to see them at home. I wouldn't bother about that, said Bob, I think the trip would be interesting and I think you'd better take it. And take it I did. It was a wonderful experience. And I really pretty well forgot about Germany and the Germans in the enormous pleasure of living intimately with the American Army.

We got into the 441st Troop Carrier airplane Duke II. There had been a Duke 1st but Dick Worl our small lively pilot had fought her to a finish, and now here was Duke II big enough to carry a jeep beside ourselves, three lieutenants and nine enlisted men. We wanted to give as many a good time as we could.

It was an unfailing pleasure wherever we went to see any officer in Germany divided between consternation and awe when I said I want billets and mess and transport for Miss Toklas, myself, three lieutenants and nine enlisted men. It was like an Oriental pasha and his tail, and wherever we went they all went and we didn't ever have to take out our jeep, the officers were so impressed everywhere they gave us all the transport we wanted. I like that word transport, we were transported in every sense of the word.

Alright we were in Dreux they inducted us into the plane after the jeep was pushed and pulled in, and the doors were closed, we were all inside and went up, up into the solid air. I like that solid air.

We hummed along not too high and a beautiful blue sky and we were all looking and soon it was Germany and then John Roessel the navigator came and said here is the Rhine, and there was the dirty Rhine, I had seen it when I was 19 years old on a vacation and that was long ago. We were all excited and then before we knew it we were down in Frankfort, and hungry. You get awfully hungry flying, yes you do.

We were enthusiastically received and the boys wanted me to eat with them and eat with them I did, it was good and plenty. Then after considerable conversation, there always is that in the Army, photographing and autographing we had the cars and off we all went to see Germany, we had seen it ruined from the air and now we saw it ruined on the ground. It certainly is ruined, and not so exciting to look at, I had seen ruins in France before, but the people were strange, very well dressed, was it that they all had on their best clothes because they had nothing else to wear, and shoes, did they not know what the French knew so well, better wear your old clothes and keep your best for later on or didn't they have any old clothes, and were there no working men, nobody who worked with their hands. I was puzzled.

I had noticed that they turned their heads away and tried not to look at the endless forward and back of the American Army, and then once when we had all gotten out to look at something, I began to realize that they were all looking at Miss Toklas and myself and that some went quite pale and others looked furious. First I was puzzled and then I realized that we were probably the very first ordinary civilian women with American soldiers, not looking official just looking like American women with a group of talking soldiers, and they realized for the first time that there were going to be thousands of civilians coming there just to look as we were looking. After all Germans believe in an army, an army is an army even if it is a conquering army but civilians, just simple civilians, oh dear. I thought perhaps I was imagining this but later on several of the boys spoke of it. When I was back in Paris I mentioned it to my French friends, and they said yes, that had happened in Paris, the army of occupation that was bad enough but when the German families began to come then the iron entered their French souls. Civilians are more permanent and appalling than any army, yes they are.

We drove around and around, everybody had told me that the Germans looked well fed, well yes in a way, but, and eyes trained by four years of occupation, I noticed that the men's clothes did not quite fit them, they were beginning to hang, the women did not yet show anything, the children a little, but as I found out in France, it is men from 30 on, who give you the first indication that they are undernourished. Was I pleased to see it, well a little yes.

When General Osborne came to see me just after the victory, he asked me what I thought should be done to educate the Germans. I said there is only one thing to be done and that is to teach them disobedience, as long as they are obedient so long sooner or later they will be ordered about by a bad man and there will be trouble.

Teach them disobedience, I said, make every German child know that it is its duty at least once a day to do its good deed and not believe something its father or its teacher tells them, confuse their minds, get their minds confused and perhaps then they will be disobedient and the world will be at peace. The obedient peoples go to war, disobedient peoples like peace, that is the reason that Italy did not really become a good Axis, the people were not obedient enough, the Japs and the Germans are the only really obedient people on earth and see what happens, teach them disobedience, confuse their minds, teach them disobedience, and the world can be peaceful.

General Osborne shook his head sadly, you'll never make the heads of an army understand that.

Well anyway it was almost four in the afternoon and we went back to the airport, back to America and Americans.

Before taking off again for Cologne we went around the airport to see the different crowds. Among others there was a Negro battalion and there Victor Joell quoted my poetry to me, that gave me a lot of pleasure, it was the first time in this war that that happened. Enough said. Another thing. Negroes even those born and bred and schooled in the South, don't talk with a Southern accent any more. Why is that.

Well we took off and went up the Rhine to Cologne, we flew low over and over Cologne and then we found that the airports there were not functioning so we went on to Coblenz where they were not functioning either and so back to Frankfort. Cologne was the most destroyed city we had seen yet, it is natural, of course it is natural to speak of one's roof, roofs are in a way the most important thing in a house, between four walls, under a roof, and here was a whole spread out city without a roof. There was the cathedral but it looked very fragile as if you pushed it hard with your finger your finger either would go through or it would fall over.

The next morning we left for Salzburg. There we were most hospitably received and off we went to visit Hitler and Goering, that is their homes and their stolen treasure.

When we got into Berchtesgaden I was surprised so were we all to see it such a summer resort village and not at all isolated or mysterious, we soon came to the house where Goering's works of art were temporarily housed, here there was a little trouble because only officers could go in and the only one of the crowd who was really interested in pictures was a corporal, but finally that was permitted.

You see it is natural that I see many more enlisted men than officers, that is natural enough. Anybody interested in art or literature almost automatically does not become an officer, he is either a private or a noncommissioned officer, they mostly are noncommissioned officers. That is natural enough, the kind of training, the responsibility and burden of rank, which is upon any lieutenant does not suit the other temperament, that is natural enough, beside anyway even the enlisted men who are not particularly interested in the arts their minds move more freely than the officers who have all that compression put upon them and their minds have to be extraordinarily free if they are not going to be hardened into something quite unelastic.

It is natural quite natural that I gravitate naturally to the society of the enlisted men.

It was exciting to see all those pictures but it had nothing in particular to do with Goering, there was no personal taste, he had excellent advice apparently. The only thing that might have been a personal taste were the very big landscapes, well it was very exciting, just like playing with a museum and discovering your pictures, as nothing was *expertised,* some very interesting French stuff, practically no Italian, it was exciting but strangely enough not as Goering but just as pictures stacked on the floor against the wall.

And then we all climbed into our transport, that is our cars and off we went to Hitler. That was exciting. It was exciting to be there, the other houses were bombed but Hitler's was not it was burned but not down and there we were in that big window where Hitler dominated the world a bunch of GIs just gay and happy. It really was the first time I saw our boys really gay and careless, really forgetting their burdens and just being foolish kids, climbing up and around and on top, while Miss Toklas and I sat comfortably and at home on garden chairs on Hitler's balcony. It was funny it was completely funny, it was more than funny it was absurd and yet so natural. We all got together and pointed as Hitler had pointed but mostly we just sat while they climbed around. And then they began to hunt souvenirs, they found photographs and some X-ray photographs that they were convinced were taken of Hitler's arm after the attempt on his life. What I wanted was a radiator, Hitler did have splendid radiators, and there was one all alone which nobody seemed to notice but a radiator a large radiator, what could I do with it, they asked, put it on a terrace and grow flowers over it, I said, but our courage was not equal to the weight of it and we sadly left it behind us. After we had played around till it was late off we went, down the hills and that day was over, it was a wonderful day.

We had dinner with the men of the 101st Airborne Division, our boys the carriers had dropped them to where they went several times and then home to the hotel.

There we did have trouble locating our bags. Sometimes I would get impatient with the boys and say well now for Heaven's sake let's have a little civilian efficiency. Army efficiency is efficient nobody can deny, but they have so many men that there are always ten to do what two do in civilian life and so of course you always have to find out if all ten have done it instead of just the two, which does, well which just does. Anybody in the Army can tell you that and we were in the Army for four days.

Finally with the aid of a stray colonel and a captain or two we got straightened out as to our bags and a glass of orange juice and then to bed.

The next morning we were to go to Munich and then home but there was a storm in France and Dick Worl thought it safer for us to go straight to Heidelberg and spend the night there, which we did, which did bring trouble to the *Life* office, we never knew until we got home that we changed army groups, went from the 12th to the 6th or the other way round, everybody was just as nice to us as if we had been where we belonged.

So off we went to Heidelberg and soon we were over Munich. One would suppose that every ruined town would look like any other ruined town but it does not. Munich with all its big open spaces gardens and stadiums and everything looked not so much ruined as dilapidated, it looked completely dilapidated, as if in a few years it would just sort of not exist. And then Dick turned me over to Ernest Thomas and he was a good teacher and I drove over Nuremberg around and around. He was a very good teacher and it is very like steering a ship, has nothing at all to do with an automobile, it was like when the captain used to let my brother and myself as children steer the ferryboat in upper San Francisco Bay. Nuremberg again was different, it was more nonexistent, nothing really left except a piece of the old wall. Well well, printing still does go on, and then we came down in Mannheim and had transport to Heidelberg, it was two in the afternoon and we were hungry. There we were most cordially received and we even violated all Army regulations by having a real meal at three o'clock in the afternoon and it was good.

It was lovely in Heidelberg, I had been there also in a vacation once when I was at college, and it was not at all changed. We rode around the town we wandered round and it was restful. The population seemed to be leading their normal life without any particular emotion as they had in Salzburg, not at all as they had been in Frankfort, naturally not.

That evening I went over to talk to the soldiers, and to hear what they had to say, we all got very excited, Sergeant Santiani who had asked me to come complained that I confused the minds of his men, but why shouldn't their minds be confused, gracious goodness, are we going to be like the Germans, only believe in the Aryans that is our own race, a mixed race if you like but all having the same point of view. I got very angry with them, they admitted they liked the Germans better than the other Europeans. Of course you do, I said, they flatter you and they obey you, when the other countries don't like and and say so, and personally you have not been awfully ready to meet them halfway, well naturally if they don't like you they show it, the Germans don't like you but they flatter you, dog gone it, I said I bet you Fourth of July they will all be putting up our flag, and all you big babies will just be flattered to death, literally to death, I said bitterly because you will have to fight again. Well said one of them after all we are on top. Yes I said and is there any spot on earth more dangerous than on top. You don't like the Latins, or the Arabs or the Wops, or the British, well don't you forget a country can't live without friends, I want you all to get to know other countries so that you can be friends, make a little effort, try to find out what it is all about. We all got very excited, they passed me cognac, but I don't drink so they found me some grapefruit juice, and they patted me and sat me down, and there it all was.

The next morning the sergeant came over to say goodbye and gave me a card, which said to Gertie, another Radical. Bless them all.

And the next afternoon, we all were transported back to the airfield and there was a storm and we came all the way back high over the clouds and quickly, and the boys showed us all the things they had acquired. Where they had acquired, what they had acquired better not know. There are three million American soldiers there and each one of them has to have at least six souvenirs. Dear me. They call these objects liberated. This is a liberated camera. Liberated they are.

And then down we came so gently, Dick does land gently, and

there we were right back where we started from, and the boys.

You can see in the photographs how protectingly they took care of us. Bless them.

In the evening here in Paris I hear the airplanes passing over our heads, I wish we were up there in there with them. Bless them.

1945

THE NEW HOPE IN OUR
"SAD YOUNG MEN"

After the last World War there was the lost generation, they were very successful but I called them sad young men because their life was finished by 30, they dreaded their thirtieth birthday, that was the end of life for them, life began early, success was great and after 30 what was there to do, nothing. This was something that inevitably made for sadness, and it was because as a Frenchman explained, a man goes through his period of becoming civilized between 17 and 25, it is in these years that women mold him into shape, that he begins to measure himself in the real business of life against his contemporaries and competitors, he becomes civilized. The other war just destroyed that civilizing business, and they were a lost generation, their life became too easy as it did after the war was over, and life being too easy it looked as if it was over by 30 and so they were sad young men.

Everybody was so impressed by this that one of the most popular books to follow after the war was "Life Begins at Forty." The sad young men whose life had ended at 30 to their feeling needed this consolation.

And now I have been asked are the young men of this war after the war is over, are they going to be sad young men.

No I do not think so. And I do not think so for a most excellent reason, they are sad young men already, if you are sad young men then there is a fair chance that life will begin at 30 instead of ending at 30 and I think more or less that is what is going to happen to this generation.

Today is Victory Day that is the first Victory Day, the European Victory Day, and the young men are rightly told not to be too happy because it is only half over, well we certainly do believe that it is more than half over, but there has been an unconditional surrender, and remember, it was General Grant, General Ulysses Simpson Grant, who invented for America that idea of Unconditional Surrender. Ulysses Simpson Grant Unconditional Surrender Grant.

In a queer way we have come back, we Americans, to more or less the pre-Civil War state of mind. They were a sad people those pioneers, a sad faced quiet people, whose life so often began at 30

142

and at 40, so much failure so little success, life was too hard to really begin when young, you had to be old enough to really resist life in order to begin life, and then came the tremendous industrial development in America and then the facile optimism of the years roughly from Roosevelt to Roosevelt, easy wars, easy victories, easy success, easy money, easy eating and easy drinking and easy madly running around and easy publicity, easy everything.

And then came the depression and life begins at 40 and now the war and the sad young men whose life will begin at 30.

Well in a kind of way the American of the pre-Civil War and Civil War Americans who listened to Lincoln, they were more interesting than the Roosevelt to Roosevelt American, and now I am completely and entirely certain that we are going to be more interesting again, be a sad and quiet people who can listen and who can promise and who can perform.

I was so touched the other day, there was a young fellow here and we were talking about America and war, and the future and the young American said after all what have we to oppose to the world and to defend ourselves with except innocence and a kind heart. Look at the photographs of the meeting of the GI's and the Russians, yes they the GI's they have innocence and a kind heart. In the days between Roosevelt and Roosevelt they had a facile optimism to bulwark innocence and a kind heart, and in the pioneer days they had a strenuousness to bulwark themselves with to protect their innocence and their kind heart and now what have they to give themselves as a support to innocence and a kind heart.

We talk about it a lot, they talk to me about it a lot and I talk to them about it a lot and this is some of what we say.

A lot of things worry them and a lot of the things that worry them worry me. They have been away from home for two years and over and being away from home does things to you, particularly when you are away from home in an unnatural way. One thing it does, it makes people as one of our friends used to say of her mother, mother is the best Seattle realestate promoter in Europe. Yes it does do that. It makes people like that. One man said to me the other day, it's funny listening to some of the boys sell America to the French, nothing but Heaven could be like that. Yes that is one thing being away from home does to you, and the other thing is to make you doubtful, doubtful about everything about home and not home. It is, said two of them today to me it is kind of peaceful over here, they seem just kind of to do as they please they all do just kind of seem to.

143

Then lots of them who never thought very much about where their parents were born have with this prolonged contact with Europe become conscious of different countries. One of them said to me, I had no idea so many men of my generation had parents born in Europe. It has its tragic side. One fellow born in Germany who had gone to America as a little child with an older sister. When he saw those Germans in Germany, not human, not real, not conscious of being real creatures, dirty and destroyed, he said to his buddy, I have a horror of perhaps some day seeing my parents I know they must be quite as unhuman as these people, of course they are, and just think if I should run across them.

Yes the foreign background begins to come out. One day there were three of them here, one father and mother were South Italian, one father and mother Danish, one father and mother Austrian. They began to talk about eating, they all came from New York, and how they could find the specialties of their different countries in New York and how you cooked them and how you ate them.

Then of course there are the other kind of GI's who hate them all, they hate the Britishers because they hate them, they hate the French of course because they are awful, they hate the Arabs, anybody would hate Arabs and they hate the Germans of course they hate them and they even hate Russians because Russians because Russians well because Russians.

Just the same though two to four years away from home is a very long time. Just the same they say people are so much better off in America than anywhere yes they are. And then they worry about what America is going to do and what they as Americans are going to do they worry about that, and they worry whether disillusionment will help or hinder what they must do and will they be disillusioned or will they be strong in their strength, will they, they do not worry about that but they do think about that.

The minority problem worries them, they have become conscious of that too. One told me that he had an assignment with some Negro troops and he stayed with them four days. I am from California he said and I had never known Negroes and at the end of four days well I was glad in this year '45 I had not been born black. They were very nice and they were very silent one man never talked at all and their handshake was flabby. Yes, he said, they realize that a minority people makes a country divided against itself. Europe knows that, but what can we do, they say. I was with a Southern fellow a true Southerner, who likes colored men and gets along with them and in a kind of way they like him.

We were watching the prisoners being brought to the station in trucks from the airfield. There were a number of Negroes and the French populace who were standing around to greet them and to help them put up their hands to help them down the tired men and to take their bundles and help, and the white and the black hands were all equally happy to be helped and to be helping all mingled together. We stood by watching and the Southerner said, could you see that in any city in the United States. Well I said you see to the French any soldier of France is as good as any other soldier, the flag hallows them. Yes I know he said. They tried to propagandize, the Germans did, that French women all married Negroes. They don't. The Negroes marry mostly among themselves I know that now but the French do treat them naturally, yes they do.

He went on talking. I said the trouble is, as long as the Negro was just a native race, the white man's burden point of view, it's all right, but now when one Negro can write as Richard Wright does writing as a Negro about Negroes, writes not as a Negro, but as a man, well the minute that happens the relation between the white and the Negro is no longer a difference of races but a minority question and ends not in ownership but in persecution. That is the trouble, when people have no equality there can be differences but no persecution, when they begin to have equality, then it is no longer separation there is persecution.

A good many of the boys begin to know what the words imprisoned and persecution mean, when they see the millions in prison, imprisoned for years, persecuted for years, they begin to realize what minorities in a country are bound to lead to, to persecution and to a sense of imprisonment. When these American boys see all the instability of a whole continent imprisoned as the whole of Europe has been in prison, well somehow it does something to them, of course it does.

God bless them, innocence and a kind heart, yes they will go on, innocence and a kind heart, it worries them, they are troubled, so am I, life will begin at 30 for them, so really did mine, I like them, they like me, we are American. Bless them.

1945

WHY I LIKE DETECTIVE STORIES

Life said Edgar is neither long nor short, and anybody knows that the only detective stories that anybody can read are written by Edgar. When Gerald Berners was here and his chauffeur William they both wanted detective stories, I gave William Edgar Wallace, he wanted Edgar Wallace, I cannot say that Gerald Berners did, but then he might have, anyway I had them to give them and I always find a new one by him, you might think other people wrote them but finally you know better, you finally do know that all the Edgar Wallace stories are written by him.

What are detective stories, well detective stories are what I can read. You are always finding a new author and each one makes you very enthusiastic, and then you get used to it and on the whole like to read them over again, there are the Coles and Farjeon. Farjeon is very good, he tries to be as good as Edgar Wallace but in a kind of a way it is always a mistake to try. On the whole I think English ones better than American ones, they are more long winded which is better and money is more real in them which is very much better.

Here is a little conversation about them. It is called *Money Is Not Money*.

Money is not money said Edgar to Edgar. What do you mean by that said Edgar, I mean by that said Edgar that money is not money if you do not owe money to another. Oh yes yes said Edgar. But you always do you do always owe money to another, no said Edgar. No.

It was Thursday and they said this to each other on Thursday. On Friday they said it again. Edgar said that money is not money if you do not have to give money to somebody else. Suppose said Edgar you owe yourself money then it is not money, oh yes it is said Edgar. Edgar did nt listen to Edgar because he know better than Edgar.

So then Saturday came and then Sunday. Edgar went out in the evening, he had been out in the afternoon and he went out in the evening. So did Edgar. They met and they talked together and they talked about it, Edgar said I tell you money is not money if you do not owe it to another, now he said listen, a father of course

146

if he has children he is a father, a father if he stops the allowance of his children the children if they have to spend it have to get it and so they get it from their father. You see said Edgar children cannot steal from their father that is french law, a father cannot accuse his children of stealing from him not according to french law so if the father does not give the money to his children then the children can take it from the father and it is not money until they pay it to someone else. That is what Edgar said to Edgar and after that Edgar said that they need hours to think about that and then they settled to go away. Edgar went and after that Edgar went away. It made them go one at a time.

You see that is the reason why money has to be, otherwise a detective story could not be interesting. Edgar Wallace makes it mysterious but it is always money, it is a disappointment when it is drugs or an international conspiracy, you always have the feeling that all the struggle is not worth while because by the time the real war comes all that diplomacy will have been forgotten and so what is the use and drugs that is the same, just about the same quantity of drugs get in anyway, but money that is different, twenty guineas is different, money is different and English people do feel that money is more real than Americans feel it is and that is why their detective stories are so much more soothing.

I used to think that a detective story was soothing because the hero being dead, you begin with the corpse you did not have to take him on and so your mind was free to enjoy yourself, of course there is the detection but nobody really believes in detection, that is what makes the detection so soothing, they try to make you believe in the detection by trying to make you fond of the character that does the detecting, they know if you do not get fond of him you will not believe in the detection, naturally not and you have to believe in it a little or else it will not be soothing. I like detecting there are so many things to detect, why did somebody say what they said, why did somebody cut out a paragraph in the proof I was correcting, why did the young man we were to meet at the station and whom we have never seen before not turn up and why did they telephone to somebody else that he was still at the station waiting for us and why when we got there could nobody find him neither the fat porter nor the thin one and certainly it was a very small station and finally why when we had all given him up and we were starting for home did I find him on the other side of the station and where had he been. He never did tell us but I detected the reason it was because he resembled some one else who might

147

have done it although the other one never had.

Really why Edgar Wallace is so good is that there is no detection. He makes it ordinary and the ordinary because he is genuinely romantic has an extraordinary charm. The girl will always be caught by the villain just before the end and the chase is to end only in one way that is in the rescue and sometime he has to cudgel his brains to find some reason for this capture of the heroine but captured she is and it is a charm. Moreover and of course that is the important moreover there can be in any of his books lots of them lots of everybody but there does not ever have to be a dead one it is like a good play of Shakespeare, have them dead but if they are dead then the place is strewn with corpses, but and that is the real reason why Edgar Wallace holds is because his books are strewn with people with plans with everything as well as with corpses there is a genuine abundance and the thing that can be said is characteristic of the twentieth century is that it is lavish but niggardly. Oppenheim is that but Edgar Wallace never, from the first *People of the River* to the last chase for the girl there is abundance, of course incidentally he writes awfully well he has the gift of writing as Walter Scott had it and that too makes for abundance. I like Edgar Wallace. For many years his sadism put me off as Dickens' sadism put me off but finally you have to conclude that English abundance has to have that and alright I like abundance.

They say that there are an awful lot of detective stories written but really there are not really not, if you want to read one a day well not one a day but one every other day, say three a week and if you are willing to read over and over a lot of them even then there are not enough to go around if you include English and American ones, really there are not I can say in all sincerity that there are not.

I tried to write one well not exactly write one because to try is to cry but I did try to write one.

It had a good name it was *Blood on the Dining-Room Floor* and it all had to do with that but there was no corpse and the detecting was general, it was all very clear in my head but it did not get natural the trouble was that if it all happened and it all had happened then you had to mix it up with other things that had happened and after all a novel even if it is a detective story ought not to mix up what happened with what has happened, anything that has happened is exciting exciting enough without any writing, tell it as often as you like but do not write it not as a story.

However I did write it, it was such a good detective story but nobody did any detecting except just conversation so after all it was not a detective story so finally I concluded that even although Edgar Wallace does almost write detective stories without anybody really doing any detecting on the whole a detective story has to have if it has not a detective it has to have an ending and my detective story did not have any.

I was sorry about it because it came so near to being a detective story and it did have a good title. Anyway finally I did write two very little ones, all about the same time, one was called *A Piano and a Waterfall* the other one was called *Is Dead,* but there was no detective hero there were corpses but no detecting and there was money but that was there completely separated from what had been happening, if you have no motive and no detecting can it be a detective story I can only hope so because I would really and truly like to write one.

And so it comes to this the best detective story writer Edgar Wallace does not really have any detecting and it does not begin with a corpse, there are often plenty of corpses or nearly corpses but they are usually incidental corpses, the really important people come to be corpses sometime but not necessarily while you are reading, most generally not, the only thing you have to do in an Edgar Wallace story is to detect the villain, the villain naturally is a criminal but that is only incidental he is a villain entirely but that is entirely a different thing, and the hero is nothing but a hero, his detecting is incidental and the heroine is a heroine because inevitably there is a rescue. Edgar Wallace quite rightly uses the old melodrama machinery ánd he makes it alive again and that is everything it is much better to make an old thing alive than to invent a new one anybody can know that.

So then there seems to be only two things to do one of the things, you either use the old melodrama scheme or you use the Sherlock Holmes super-detective and the crime and the criminal is nothing but something for the unreal hero to conquer. I do not wish to be ungrateful to the Sherlock Holmes kind but I guess I do like the melodrama best, the melodrama scheme gives more abundance than the one hero kind. In the melodrama the three are equal the villain th hero and the heroine, in this order as to importance but nevertheless they all three have the right to be but in the detective hero type the rest of it becomes too dependent and eventually the hero detective having really to exist all by himself ceases to exist at all. I am not ungrateful for that kind I like them but there it is they do have that failing.

There are also the detective stories of Fletcher, there it all depends not upon the criminal not upon the detecting but upon the crime, and the crime is money money is there sometimes as diamonds mostly uncut sometimes cut but it all depends entirely upon the crime, crime and ancient history which explains the crime, here there is neither hero nor villain and certainly not a heroine there is only the crime.

It is funny that crime is soothing but it is, stories of adventure criminals, the kind they used to write about Australian bushrangers were more likely to frighten you than crimes of criminals, I do not know why but this is so. Criminal crimes are soothing, adventure crimes are frightening. I suppose because criminal crimes take place where there are lots of people and adventure crimes take place where there are none. Anyway I do like detective stories and will there please will there be more of them.

1937

HOW WRITING IS WRITTEN

What I want to talk about to you tonight is just the general subject of how writing is written. It is a large subject, but one can discuss it in a very short space of time. The beginning of it is what everybody has to know: everybody is contemporary with his period. A very bad painter once said to a very great painter, "Do what you like, you cannot get rid of the fact that we are contemporaries." That is what goes on in writing. The whole crowd of you are contemporary to each other, and the whole business of writing is the question of living in that contemporariness. Each generation has to live in that. The thing that is important is that nobody knows what the contemporariness is. In other words, they don't know where they are going, but they are on their their way.

Each generation has to do with what you would call the daily life: and a writer, painter, or any sort of creative artist, is not at all ahead of his time. He is contemporary. He can't live in the past, because it is gone. He can't live in the future because no one knows what it is. He can live only in the present of his daily life. He is expressing the thing that is being expressed by everybody else in their daily lives. The thing you have to remember is that everybody lives a contemporary daily life. The writer lives it, too, and expresses it imperceptibly. The fact remains that in the act of living, everybody has to live contemporarily. But in the things concerning art and literature they don't have to live contemporarily, because it doesn't make any difference; and they live about forty years behind their time. And that is the real explanation of why the artist or painter is not recognized by his contemporaries. He is expressing the time-sense of his contemporaries, but nobody is really interested. After the new generation has come, after the grandchildren, so to speak, then the opposition dies out: because after all there is then a new contemporary expression to oppose.

That is really the fact about contemporariness. As I see the whole crowd of you, if there are any of you who are going to express yourselves contemporarily, you will do something which most people won't want to look at. Most of you will be so busy living the contemporary life that it will be like the tired businessman: in the things of the mind you will want the things you know. And too, if

151

you don't live contemporarily, you are a nuisance. That is why we live contemporarily. If a man goes along the street with horse and carriage in New York in the snow, that man is a nuisance; and he know it, so now he doesn't do it. He would not be living, or acting, contemporarily: he would only be in the way, a drag.

The world can accept me now because there is coming out of your generation somebody they don't like, and therefore they accept me because I am sufficiently past in having been contemporary so they don't have to dislike me. So thirty years from now I shall be accepted. And the same thing will happen again: that is the reason why every generation has the same thing happen. It will always be the same story, because there is always the same situation presented. The contemporary thing in art and literature is the thing which doesn't make enough difference to the people of that generation so that they can accept it or reject it.

Most of you know that in a funny kind of way you are nearer your grandparents than your parents. Since this contemporariness is always there, nobody realizes that you cannot follow it up. That is the reason people discover—those interested in the activities of other people—that they cannot understand their contemporaries. If you kids started in to write, I wouldn't be a good judge of you, because I am of the third generation. What you are going to do I don't know any more than anyone else. But I created a movement of which you are the grandchildren. The contemporary thing is the thing you can't get away from. That is the fundamental thing in all writing.

Another thing you have to remember is that each period of time not only has its contemporary quality, but it has a time-sense. Things move more quickly, slowly, or differently, from one generation to another. Take the Nineteenth Century. The Nineteenth Century was roughly the Englishman's Century. And their method, as they themselves, in their worst moments, speak of it, is that of "muddling through". They begin at one end and hope to come out at the other: their grammar, parts of speech, methods of talk, go with this fashion. The United States began a different phase when, after the Civil War, they discovered and created out of their inner need a different way of life. They created the Twentieth Century. The United States, instead of having the feeling of beginning at one end and ending at another, had the conception of assembling the whole thing out of its parts, the whole thing which made the Twentieth Century productive. The Twentieth Century conceived an automobile as a whole, so to speak, and then created it, built it up out of its parts. It was an entirely different point of view from the Nineteenth Century's. The Nineteenth Century would have seen the parts, and worked towards the automobile through them.

Now in a funny sort of way this expresses, in different terms, the difference between the literature of the Nineteenth Century and the literature of the Twentieth. Think of your reading. If you look at it from the days of Chaucer, you will see that what you might call the "internal history" of a country always affects its use of writing. It makes a difference in the expression, in the vocabulary, even in the handling of grammar. In Vanderbilt's amusing story in your *Literary Magazine*, when he speaks of the fact that he is tired of using quotation marks and isn't going to use them any more, with him that is a joke; but when I began writing, the whole question of punctuation was a vital question. You see, I had this new conception: I had this conception of the whole paragraph, and in *The Making of Americans* I had this idea of a whole thing. But if you think of contemporary English writers, it doesn't work like that at all. They conceive of it as pieces put together to make a whole, and I conceived it as a whole made up of its parts. I didn't know what I was doing any more than you know, but in response to the need of my period I was doing this thing. That is why I came in contact with people who were unconsciously doing the same thing. They had the Twentieth Century conception of a whole. So the element of punctuation was very vital. The comma was just a nuisance. If you got the thing as a whole, the comma kept irritating you all along the line. If you think of a thing as a whole, and the comma keeps sticking out, it gets on your nerves; because, after all, it destroys the reality of the whole. So I got rid more and more of commas. Not because I had any prejudice against commas; but the comma was a stumbling block. When you were conceiving a sentence, the comma stopped you. That is the illustration of the question of grammar and parts of speech, as part of the daily life as we live it.

The other thing which I accomplished was the getting rid of nouns. In the Twentieth Century you feel like movement. The Nineteenth Century didn't feel that way. The element of movement was not the predominating thing that they felt. You know that in your lives movement is the thing that occupies you most—you feel movement all the time. And the United States had the first instance of what I call Twentieth Century writing. You see it first in Walt Whitman. He was the beginning of the movement. He didn't see it very clearly, but there was a sense of movement that the European was much influenced by, because the Twentieth Century has be-

153

come the American Century. That is what I mean when I say that each generation has its own literature.

There is a third element. You see, everybody in his generation has his sense of time which belongs to his crowd. But then, you always have the memory of what you were brought up with. In most people that makes a double time, which makes confusion. When one is beginning to write he is always under the shadow of the thing that is just past. And that is the reason why the creative person always has the appearance of ugliness. There is this persistent drag of the habits that belong to you. And in struggling away from this thing there is always an ugliness. That is the other reason why the contemporary writer is always refused. It is the effort of escaping from the thing which is a drag upon you that is so strong that the result is an apparent ugliness; and the world always says of the new writer, "It is so ugly!" And they are right, because it *is* ugly. If you disagree with your parents, there is an ugliness in the relation. There is a double resistance that makes the essence of this thing ugly.

You always have in your writing the resistance outside of you and inside of you, a shadow upon you, and the thing which you must express. In the beginning of your writing, this struggle is so tremendous that the result is ugly; and that is the reason why the followers are always accepted before the person who made the revolution. The person who has made the fight probably makes it seem ugly, although the struggle has the much greater beauty. But the followers die out; and the man who made the struggle and the quality of beauty remains in the intensity of the fight. Eventually it comes out all right, and so you have this very queer situation which always happens with the followers: the original person has to have in him a certain element of ugliness. You know that is what happens over and over again: the statement made that it is ugly—the statement made against me for the last twenty years. And they are quite right, because it *is* ugly. But the essence of that ugliness is the thing which will always make it beautiful. I myself think it is much more interesting when it seems ugly, because in it you see the element of the fight. The literature of one hundred years ago is perfectly easy to see, because the sediment of ugliness has settled down and you get the solemnity of its beauty. But to a person of my temperament, it is much more amusing when it has the vitality of the struggle.

In my own case, the Twentieth Century, which America created after the Civil War, and which had certain elements, had a definite influence on me. And in *The Making of Americans*, which is a book I would like to talk about, I gradually and slowly found out that there were two things I had to think about; the fact that knowledge is acquired, so to speak, by memory; but that when you know anything, memory doesn't come in. At any moment that you are conscious of knowing anything, memory plays no part. When any of you feels anybody else, memory doesn't come into it. You have the sense of the immediate. Remember that my immediate forebears were people like Meredith, Thomas Hardy, and so forth, and you will see what a struggle it was to do this thing. This was one of my first efforts to give the appearance of one time-knowledge, and not to make it a narrative story. This is what I mean by immediacy of description: you will find it in *The Making of Americans*, on page 284: "It happens very often that a man has it in him, that a man does something, that he does it very often that he does many things, when he is a young man when he is an old man, when he is an older man." Do you see what I mean? And here is a description of a thing that is very interesting: "One of such of these kind of them had a little boy and this one, the little son wanted to make a collection of butterflies and beetles and it was all exciting to him and it was all arranged then and then the father said to the son you are certain this is not a cruel thing that you are wanting to be doing, killing things to make collections of them, and the son was very disturbed then and they talked about it together the two of them and more and more they talked about it then and then at last the boy was convinced it was a cruel thing and he said he would not do it and the father said the little boy was a noble boy to give up pleasure when it was a cruel one. The boy went to bed then and then the father when he got up in the early morning saw a wonderfully beautiful moth in the room and he caught him and he killed him and he pinned him and he woke up his son then and showed it to him and he said to him 'see what a good father I am to have caught and killed this one,' the boy was all mixed up inside him and then he said he would go on with his collection and that was all there was then of discussing and this is a little description of something that happened once and it is very interesting."

I was trying to get this present immediacy without trying to drag in anything else. I had to use present participles, new constructions of grammar. The grammar-constructions are correct, but they are changed, in order to get this immediacy. In short, from that time I have been trying in every possible way to get the sense of immediacy, and practically all the work I have done has been in that

155

direction.

In *The Making of Americans* I had an idea that I could get a sense of immediacy if I made a description of every kind of human being that existed, the rules for resemblances and all the other things, until really I had made a description of every human being—I found this out when I was at Harvard working under William James.

Did you ever see that article that came out in *The Atlantic Monthly* a year or two ago, about my experiments with automatic writing? It was very amusing. The experiment that I did was to take a lot of people in moments of fatigue and rest and activity of various kinds, and see if they could do anything with automatic writing. I found that they could not do anything with automatic writing, but I found out a great deal about how people act. I found there a certain kind of human being who acted in a certain way, and another kind who acted in another kind of way, and their resemblances and their differences. And then I wanted to find out if you could make a history of the whole world, if you could know the whole life history of everyone in the world, their slight resemblances and lack of resemblances. I made enormous charts, and I tried to carry these charts out. You start in and you take everyone that you know, and then when you see anybody who has a certain expression or turn of the face that reminds you of some one, you find out where he agree or disagrees with the character, until you build up the whole scheme. I got to the place where I didn't know whether I knew people or not. I made so many charts that when I used to go down the streets of Paris I wondered whether they were people I knew or ones I didn't. That is what *The Making of Americans* was intended to be. I was to make a description of every kind of human being until I could know by these variations how everybody was to be known. Then I got very much interested in this thing, and I wrote about nine hundred pages, and I came to a logical conclusion that this thing could be done. Anybody who has patience enough could literally and entirely make of the whole world a history of human nature. When I found it could be done, I lost interest in it. As soon as I found definitely and clearly and completely that I could do it, I stopped writing the long book. It didn't interest me any longer. In doing the thing, I found out this question of resemblances, and I found in making these analyses that the resemblances were not of memory. I had to remember what person looked like the other person. Then I found this contradiction: that the resemblances were a matter of memory.

156

There were two prime elements involved, the element of memory and the other of immediacy.

The element of memory was a perfectly feasible thing, so then I gave it up. I then started a book which I called *A Long Gay Book* to see if I could work the thing up to a faster tempo. I wanted to see if I could make that a more complete vision. I wanted to see if I could hold it in the frame. Ordinarily the novels of the Nineteenth Century live by association; they are wont to call up other pictures than the one they present to you. I didn't want, when I said "water", to have you think of running water. Therefore I began by limiting my vocabulary, because I wanted to get rid of anything except the picture within the frame. While I was writing I didn't want, when I used one word, to make it carry with it too many associations. I wanted as far as possible to make it exact, as exact as mathematics; that is to say, for example, if one and one make two, I wanted to get words to have as much exactness as that. When I put them down they were to have this quality. The whole history of my work, from *The Making of Americans*, has been a history of that. I made a great many discoveries, but the thing that I was always trying to do was this thing.

One thing which came to me is that the Twentieth Century gives of itself a feeling of movement, and has in its way no feeling for events. To the Twentieth Century events are not important. You must know that. Events are not exciting. Events have lost their interest for people. You read them more like a soothing syrup, and if you listen over the radio you don't get very excited. The thing has got to this place, that events are so wonderful that they are not exciting. Now you have to remember that the business of an artist is to be exciting. If the thing has its proper vitality, the result must be exciting. I was struck with it during the War: the average dough-boy standing on a street corner doing nothing— (they say, at the end of their doing nothing, "I guess I'll go home")—was much more exciting to people than when the soldiers went over the top. The populace were passionately interested in their standing on the street corners, more so than in the St. Mihiel drive. And it is a perfectly natural thing. Events had got so continuous that the fact that events were taking place no longer stimulated anybody. To see three men, strangers, standing, expressed their personality to the European man so much more than anything else they could do. That thing impressed me very much. But the novel which tells about what happens is of no interest to anybody. It is quite characteristic that in *The Making of Americans*, Proust,

157

Ulysses, nothing much happens. People are interested in existence. Newspapers excite people very little. Sometimes a personality breaks through the newspapers—Lindbergh, Dillinger—when the personality has vitality. It wasn't what Dillinger *did* that excited anybody. The feeling is perfectly simple. You can see it in my *Four Saints*. Saints shouldn't do anything. The fact that a saint is there is enough for anybody. The *Four Saints* was written about as static as I could make it. The saints conversed a little, and it all did something. It did something more than the theatre which has tried to make events has done. For our purposes, for our contemporary purposes, events have no importance. I merely say that for the last thirty years events are of no importance. They make a great many people unhappy, they may cause convulsions in history, but from the standpoint of excitement, the kind of excitement the Nineteenth Century got out of events doesn't exist.

And so what I am trying to make you understand is that every contemporary writer has to find out what is the inner time-sense of his contemporariness. The writer or painter, or what not, feels this thing more vibrantly, and he has a passionate need of putting it down; and that is what creativeness does. He spends his life in putting down this thing which he doesn't know is a contemporary thing. If he doesn't put down the contemporary thing, he isn't a great writer, for he has to live in the past. That is what I mean by "everything is contemporary". The minor poets of the period, or the precious poets of the period, are all people who are under the shadow of the past. A man who is making a revolution has to be contemporary. A minor person can live in the imagination. That tells the story pretty completely.

The question of repetition is very important. It is important because there is no such thing as repetition. Everybody tells every story in about the same way. You know perfectly well that when you and your roommates tell something, you are telling the same story in about the same way. But the point about it is this. Everybody is telling the story in the same way. But if you listen carefully, you will see that not all the story is the same. There is always a slight variation. Somebody comes in and you tell the story over again. Every time you tell the story it is told slightly differently. All my early work was a careful listening to all the people telling their story, and I conceived the idea which is, funnily enough, the same as the idea of the cinema. The cinema goes on the same principle: each picture is just infinitesimally different from the one before. If you listen carefully, you say something, the other person says something; but each time it changes just a little, until finally you come to the point where you convince him or you don't convince him. I used to listen very carefully to people talking. I had a passion for knowing just what I call their "insides". And in *The Making of Americans* I did this thing; but of course to my mind there is no repetition. For instance, in these early *Portraits*, and in a whole lot of them in this book (*Portraits and Prayers*) you will see that every time a statement is made about someone being somewhere, that statement is different. If I had repeated, nobody would listen. Nobody could be in the room with a person who said the same thing over and over and over. He would drive everybody mad. There has to be a very slight change. Really listen to the way you talk and every time you change it a little bit. That change, to me, was a very important thing to find out. You will see that when I kept on saying something was something or somebody was somebody, I changed it just a little bit until I got a whole portrait. I conceived the idea of building this thing up. It was all based upon this thing of everybody's slightly building this thing up. What I was after was this immediacy. A single photograph doesn't give it. I was trying for this thing, and so to my mind there is no repetition. The only thing that is repetition is when somebody tells you what he has learned. No matter how you say it, you say it differently. It was this that led me in all that early work.

You see, finally, after I got this thing as completely as I could, then, of course, it being my nature, I wanted to tear it down. I attacked the problem from another way. I listened to people. I condensed it in about three words. There again, if you read those later *Portraits*, you will see that I used three or four words instead of making a cinema of it. I wanted to condense it as much as possible and change it around, until you could get the movement of a human being. If I wanted to make a picture of you as you sit there, I would wait until I got a picture of you as individuals and then I'd change them until I got a picture of you as a whole.

I did these *Portraits*, and then I got the idea of doing plays. I had the *Portraits* so much in my head that I would almost know how you differ one from the other. I got this idea of the play, and put it down in a few words. I wanted to put them down in that way, and I began writing plays and I wrote a great many of them. The Nineteenth Century wrote a great many plays, and none of them are now read, because the Nineteenth Century wanted to put their novels on the stage. The better the play the more static. The minute you try to make a play a novel, it doesn't work. That is the reason I got interested in doing these plays.

When you get to that point there is no essential difference between prose and poetry. This is essentially the problem with which your generation will have to wrestle. The thing has got to the point where poetry and prose have to concern themselves with the static thing. That is up to you.

1935

SOURCES AND ACKNOWLEDGEMENTS

The texts as printed in this book follow the published texts (including variations between British and American spelling) except for obvious printer's errors and a few emendations in square brackets.

Thanks are given to Donald Gallup, Yale University Library, who has kindly made these sources readily available and to the Estate of Hal Levy for exerpts from the Levy MSS. Particular thanks should also go to Mr. Calman A. Levin (of Daniel C. Joseph, Literary Executor of the Gertrude Stein Estate) for his unfailing help and encouragement in this project, and to Seamus Cooney of Western Michigan University who tirelessly proofread the book against the original printed sources.

The first appearances of the material in this volume were as follows:

"Grant or Rutherford B. Hayes", *Americans Abroad*, 1932; "Page IX", *The Observer*, 1933; "Prothalamium", Joyous Guard Press, 1939; "The Superstitions of Fred Anneday, Annday, Anday", *Nassau Lit*, December 1935; "A Water-fall and A Piano", *New Directions in Prose and Poetry*, 1936; "Is Dead", *Occident*, April 1937; "Butter Will Melt", *Atlantic Monthly*, February 1937; "The Autobiography of Rose", *Partisan Review*, Winter 1939; "Ida", *Boudoir Companion*, 1938; "Why I Do Not Live in America", *Transition*, Fall 1928; "Answers to Jane Heap", *Little Review*, May 1929; "Answer to Eugene Jolas", *Transition*, March 1932; "Answers to the Partisan Review", *Partisan Review*, Summer 1939; "The Story of a Book", *Wings*, September 1933; "And Now", *Vanity Fair*, September 1934; "I Came and Here I Am", *Cosmopolitan*, February 1936; "The Capital and Capitals of The United States of America", *New York Herald Tribune*, March 9, 1935; "American States and Cities and How They Differ From Each Other", *New York Herald Tribune*, April 6, 1935; "American Food and American Houses", *New York Herald Tribune*, April 13, 1935; "American Newspapers", *New York Herald Tribune*, March 23, 1935; "American Education and Colleges", *New York Herald Tribune*, March 16, 1935; "American Crimes and How They Matter", *New York Herald Tribune*, March 30, 1935; "Money", *Saturday Evening Post*, June 13, 1936; "More About Money", *Saturday Evening Post*, July 11, 1936; "Still More About Money", *Saturday Evening Post*, July 25, 1936; "All About Money", *Saturday Evening Post*, August 22, 1936; "My Last About Money", *Saturday Evening Post*, October 10, 1936; "The Winner Loses", *Atlantic Monthly*, November 1940; "Broadcast at Voiron", (in) Eric Sevareid, *Not So Wild a Dream*, New York, 1936; "Off We All Went to See Germany", *Life*, August 6, 1945; "The New Hope in Our 'Sad Young Men'", *New York Times Magazine*, June 3, 1945; "Why I Like Detective Stories", *Harper's Bazaar* (London), November, 1937; "How Writing Is Written", *The Choate Literary Magazine*, February 1935.

Finally, the editor would like to dedicate his work on these two volumes of the Previously Uncollected Writings of Gertrude Stein to Tomi, Mariko and Reiko.